HAUNTED
WATERS

haunted waters

tales from the old coast

DICK HAMMOND

Illustrated by
Alistair Anderson

HARBOUR PUBLISHING

Published by
HARBOUR PUBLISHING
P.O. Box 219, Madeira Park, BC Canada V0N 2H0

Cover photo by Eric Boyum
Cover design, page design and composition by Martin Nichols
Illustrations by Alistair Anderson
Printed and bound in Canada

"Deer???" was first published in *Raincoast Chronicles 17*.
"Svendson and the Taxman" was first published in *Raincoast Chronicles 18*.

Harbour Publishing acknowledges the financial support of the Government of Canada through the Book Publishing Industry Development Program (BPIDP) and the Canada Council for the Arts, and the Province of British Columbia through the British Columbia Arts Council, for its publishing activities.

THE CANADA COUNCIL | LE CONSEIL DES ARTS
FOR THE ARTS | DU CANADA
SINCE 1957 | DEPUIS 1957

Canadian Cataloguing in Publication Data

Hammond, Dick, 1929–
   Haunted waters

   ISBN 1-55017-209-3

   1. Tales—British Columbia—Pacific Coast. I. Title.
PS8565.A5645H38 1999   398.2'09711'1   C99-910897-2
PR9199.3.H3244H38 1999

CONTENTS

FOREWORD

These stories were told to me by my father, Robert Henry Hammond (known as Hal.) I heard them over a span of about forty years, from childhood right up to the time he died. Some of them he told many times to many audiences, but a few of the most interesting only to me, and that reluctantly. Toward the end of his life, when I expressed interest, he went over them all with me very carefully. I still forgot much of the detail, especially names, dates and places, but the events are as he described them.

I couldn't hope to reproduce in print the full impact of his telling since, like all good tale-spinners, Father lived his stories. He acted them out with gestures, impressions, sound effects, and such running commentary as occurred to him. He imitated the sounds of different characters' voices and made valiant attempts at their accents. I have hinted at some of this, but most of his special effects I have had to leave to the readers' imagination.

I've added little except linkages and a minimum of explanation. I've employed a few devices like switching points of view and casting some of Father's first-person accounts in the third person, just for variety. But for the most part I have left him to tell his own stories in his own way.

Dick Hammond

τh∂τ's
Noτhing

I n the old days entertainment wasn't thrust upon people as it is today, and especially not in the little camps scattered about the mountain-rimmed inlets along the coast. Radios were of little or no use there, and books not readily available. So, as it had been through all the ages of human existence, they had to provide their own entertainment. At least once a week, usually on Saturday night, they would gather. There would be singing, certainly, and dancing if there was floor space enough and some sort of instrument, usually an accordion; but always there would be storytelling.

Valued was the person who could tell a good story, for not everyone possessed that skill, although it was much more common then than it is now when there is so much less need for it.

So it was not that unusual that in one small camp community in which Father stayed for a season there were no fewer than three good storytellers. One was Martin Warnock, another was a man Father called Wolf but whose last name I can't remember, and of course, Father himself. It worked out well. Stimulated by each other's presence, each did his utmost to excel, yet applauded the efforts of his friends. No one took an excessive portion of the evening, and they listened to each other's stories with due attention, even if—as was often the case—some of them had been told more than once.

Unfortunately a fly was about to come blundering into the ointment of their tranquility. A more irritating insect would be difficult to imagine, for it chose always to bite them in a place where they were particularly vulnerable!

One sunny afternoon, while Father was painting the cabin of his boat, he became conscious of a faint sound disturbing the silence. It grew suddenly louder and when he looked up from his painting he saw that a boat had rounded the point and was angling across toward the camp. He recognized the sound as that of a two-cylinder Easthope engine. It was not a happy one. Both cylinders were firing at very irregular intervals. In fact, only the momentum of the flywheel was keeping the engine going at all.

This was a particularly irksome sound to Father, for he was meticulous about keeping engines in good order, and it was with a certain amount of irritation that he heard the vessel make its uncertain way across the inlet. At last the sound eased off as with many a cough and hiccup the boat was directed toward the end of the float. But when the man at the wheel threw in the reverse and gunned the engine to bring the craft to a stop, it chose to die completely. As Father had been rather expecting this, he had walked over to the edge of the float, and as the boat slid past, he jumped on it, seized the spring line, leaped back to the float and snubbed the line on one of the wooden cleats.

When the boat was safely tied up, he looked the newcomers over. The boat he dismissed quickly as typical of its kind. Sway-backed and unpainted and in a state of general decrepitude, it immediately prejudiced him against the owner. However, he was prepared to be tolerant. There could be good reasons for the boat to be so rundown.

Along the length of the cabin ran a row of windows, and from each of the windows a child's face peered out, and in each face's mouth a thumb was inserted. "I had to look twice to be sure I wasn't seeing things," remembered Father.

The man at the wheel stepped onto the float and while introducing himself, seized Father's hand and shook it effusively. Somewhat startled, for this wasn't the custom when first meeting a stranger under these circumstances, Father eyed the newcomer closely while supplying his own name in turn. (I don't remember the man's name, but it doesn't matter, for he soon acquired a new one!)

The stranger was of about average height, thin-chested and narrow-shouldered. He had sandy-red hair and freckles, and peered defensively out at the world through eyes of a pale and faded blue. "Your engine didn't sound too good, coming in," said Father. "Having a bit of trouble with it?"

"I'm having a bit of trouble with my engine. I guess you heard it when I was coming in."

"Sounded a bit like a plugged fuel line," Father offered.

"I figure it's a plugged fuel line or something like that," came the prompt answer.

Intrigued a bit by now, Father countered with, "Or it could be the spring on the make-and-break is a bit weak."

To which the stranger replied, as if it had been his own original thought, "Of course, it could be the spring on the make-and-break is too weak."

Father wondered if the man was hard of hearing. He changed his tack. "Have you been in these waters before?"

"Oh sure. I've been all over the coast. There isn't a hole or corner that I don't know like the back of my hand."

"That's what I thought," agreed Father, "when you went between the rocks off the point. A man has to know what he's doing to go through there like that."

The stranger's eyes widened as he looked down the inlet, but he came back quickly with, "I guess you saw how I came through the rocks back there at the point. A man's got to know what he's doing to go through there like that."

Father grinned inwardly. He had just invented the

dangerous rocks, for the water off that point was at least a hundred feet deep. He now knew all that he cared to know about what sort of a man this was.

Now the newcomer wanted to know the name of the camp owner, and where he might be found. He explained, "I might just settle in here for a while. I'm pretty handy around a camp. Not much I can't do when I set my mind to it."

Repeating the owner's name carefully, he headed off up the road, and Father went back to his painting. He wondered idly why the children who'd been peering from the windows hadn't swarmed out to explore, and why they were so quiet. Soon, though, he heard child voices as two girls and three boys of various sizes filed out of the cabin and onto the float. Each carried a bit of stick wrapped about with fishing line. They sent wary glances his way as they gathered mussels for bait and commenced to fish from the edge of the float. There was an unchildlike air of purpose about them that puzzled him.

Their mother came out of the cabin, a thin blonde woman, rather young, he thought, to have such a brood. After one look, she took no further notice of him, but turned away to busy herself with some task in the stern of the boat.

The younger of the girls gave a short exclamation of satisfaction as she flipped a shiner onto the deck. She killed it swiftly by pinching its head, then took it to her mother, who gutted the little fish and put it carefully on a plate. The scene was repeated several times as the efforts of the others were in turn rewarded.

Father watched all this with much interest as he plied his brush. No Europeans ate the bony little fish, and Orientals only did so after pickling them in vinegar to soften the bones. "I wondered," he said, "how a man could be so short on gumption that he wouldn't throw a cod jig over the side to get food for his family."

After a bit, the newcomer came slouching back along the walk-floats. As he drew near, he announced pompously, "Well, I guess the boss knows a good man when he sees one. He hired me right there on the spot." ("Had to give him a job to get rid of him," the foreman later explained.) He sniffed loudly and appreciatively at the aroma of frying fish that was coming from his boat. "Say, you wouldn't care to join us for a bite of supper, would you?"

"No. Thanks just the same. I've eaten already," lied Father.

"I wasn't much taken by him," he told me, "but I thought he was harmless. Little did I know..."

They were given the use of a small shack set back in the trees behind the camp. The children could often be seen fishing from the shore, or picking berries. They were as shy and elusive as the feral cats that skulked about the camp. But their father was neither shy nor elusive. Quite the opposite. In fact, people were soon inventing reasons why they couldn't stop and talk with him. It wasn't easy, because he couldn't recognize even the broadest hint, and politeness was a courtesy much valued in those far-off days.

He had been given the job of woodcutter and general-purpose camp handyman, for which no one could have

been less suited, as he seemed to have no skills, save his ability to extol his own virtues, and it was no wonder he was good at that, he got so much practice at it! For example, he caught Father at his boat one day not long after they had arrived.

"Say, Hal," he began, "I wonder if you'd have a look at my engine? I'd fix it myself, but I loaned my tools to someone and never got them back."

"Oh well, you'll probably only need a screwdriver and a wrench. You can use mine if you like."

"Oh no, I couldn't do that." And then, virtuously, "I never use any tools but my own. Wouldn't think of it."

So Father took a handful of tools and went to have a look. The trouble was easy enough to find. The fuel settling bowl was full of dirt and water, obviously having not been cleaned for a very long time. But all the time he worked on the engine, Father had to listen to a long and unlikely account of the fantastically complicated steam engine which the man had fixed when no one else could.

"It wasn't so much that I minded being lied to. No, it was him thinking I was stupid enough to swallow that story, when he couldn't even clean out his own fuel line!"

But the real irritation caused by the newcomer became apparent only slowly, and involved the ritual of storytelling. As a matter of course, he and his wife were invited to the weekly gatherings, and he accepted with the greatest alacrity. When the time came he was right there, with his wife behind him. She was a quiet woman who fitted in well enough, although she never seemed to have much to say. She answered the questions of the other women politely but seldom volunteered anything of her own. Her mate, however, was not so retiring. After piling a plate high with the best of whatever refreshments were offered, he would drag a chair to a prominent place in the room and wait to be entertained. His goal was for someone to tell a story. Not just any story. What he was waiting for was a story that was about something of note: a large fish, or a quantity of game. Anything involving size was what he liked best. As soon as the story was finished, he would announce in a loud voice, "That's nothing!" and proceed to top it with some poorly told recitation of how he caught a bigger fish, killed a fiercer bear or a fatter buck, or made a better shot than the one he had just heard about. And he was soon known to the three increasingly irritated storytellers (who were his chief victims) by his favourite phrase, "That's nothing."

Now, it was not that they didn't occasionally try to "top" one another's stories. Far from it. But the words "that's nothing" do not have a nice ring to them. Moreover, the stories he told were so obviously false, and their narrator so obviously incapable of the exploits he invented, that Father and his friends found very little room in their hearts for charity. And finally there came an evening that was just too much for them.

They were all gathered in the living room of the camp "super." The evening was young, the conversation general. Earlier that day Father had walked up the valley looking for deer. He hadn't seen any, but did manage to bring back four grouse.

His friend Wolf spoke up. "Nice bunch of grouse you got, Hal," and to the room at large, "Anyone that saw those grouse would think it was pretty good shooting. Each one with the head shot off. The fact is, though, it's that gun of his. He just has to point that old 38/55 in the general direction and pull the trigger. The gun does all the rest. Can't miss!"

Though it was still early and the storytelling was not underway, this was too much for the man with the plate full of food. He couldn't resist such an opportunity. Out he burst with his declaimer.

"That's nothing!" He went on, "I don't call that particularly good shooting, is it, Mabel?" to his wife, who was sitting quietly in the corner.

"No dear," she answered.

"Now, where I come from up the coast, we don't fool around with a half dozen birds or so, do we, Mabel?"

"No dear."

"When I used to go after grouse, do you know what I'd do first? What I'd do first is look up a couple of gunny sacks. Big ones. Isn't that right, Mabel?"

"Yes dear."

"Then I'd throw a couple of boxes of shells in my pocket and off I'd go. I use a .22 for grouse. Costs too much for rifle bullets the amount of grouse we used to get. Then I'd go and get my friend. There was only one man I'd go hunting with. The rest weren't good enough shots. He was almost as good as me. Not quite, but almost. Isn't that right, Mabel?"

"Yes dear."

"We'd just be gone a couple of hours, no more. There's lots of grouse up there if you know where to go. We'd come back with the sacks full, just about all that a man could carry. I'd dump the sacks out on the ground and I'd say, 'Mabel, come and pick out my birds.' And she would every time. And you know how she did it? She just took the ones that were shot in the eye. The right eye." He paused complacently. "There was one time she almost made a mistake. She picked this grouse up, put it down, then picked it up again. Then she threw it down. 'No,' she said, 'that's not yours.' You see, it was shot a bit to one side of the eye, more behind the eye, so she knew that it wouldn't be mine. Isn't that right, dear?"

"Yes dear."

"Now that's what I call shooting."

The rest of the room was silent for a moment. What could one say?

As conversation began to pick up again, Father walked idly to the door. On the way he caught the eyes of the other two. Presently they joined him in the next room. He said seriously, "You know, we've got to do something about that fellow."

"That story was just too much," Martin Warnock agreed. "It wasn't even funny."

"Okay. I've got a plan that might be worth trying. You know that we've all got stories we've heard that are just too far-fetched to tell. Think up your worst or best one. I'll go first. You follow on from there, Martin. As soon as the last word leaves my lips I'll touch my chin with my finger like this so you can take over before he can get started. Then you do the same so Wolf can get going and we'll see if we can get him so worked up that he'll make a total ass of himself trying to go us one better."

"Say," objected Wolf. "You both know that all my stories are true. I might not be able to hold my end up."

"Well, from what I've heard," countered Martin, "some of them are a lot truer than others. I don't think you'll have any trouble."

One by one they drifted back into the main room. At the first appropriate opportunity, Martin Warnock—his voice rather louder than necessary—said, "Say Hal, how about giving us a good one, the kind you've been holding back because you're afraid no one will believe you. We all have some stories like that. I know I have, haven't you, Wolf?"

"Well, yes, I suppose so. Not that they're so unlikely, just a bit strange for the average person who doesn't get to do much fishing."

"So, what about it, Hal? Let's hear about your biggest trout, or the most in one day, or something like that."

Their intended victim leaned forward a bit in his chair. This was the sort of thing he waited for.

"Well," said Father to me, "you know I never exaggerate," and he grinned a bit. Whether he "stretched" a story or not depended on the audience. "But I had heard a few tall stories. I told them the one about the seven hungry fish."

"Did I ever," he asked Martin, "tell you the story about the seven trout?"

"Not that I recall, Hal."

"I'm not so sure that I should. Some people might think it was a bit far-fetched."

Everyone was listening by then. There were cries of encouragement: "Come on Hal, tell us," "We'll believe every word of it, Hal," and so on.

"Okay then, here goes. This took place in Clowhom lakes. You all know Clowhom lakes, how big the fish are there. Everyone knows about those fish. Well, I was fishing one evening just where the rapids come out of the upper lake into the lower one. I was drifting there in the skiff, right over the drop-off where the bottom shelves off into the deep water. It was that time of day when the big fish come up to feed. I was using a worm, and a little trout grabbed it and swam around with just the end of the worm in its mouth. I let it be, because it looked like pretty tempting bait itself, swimming around like that. Sure enough, pretty soon up comes a trout about nine inches long and swallows the fish, worm and hook. But that wasn't big enough to bother pulling in so I let it swim around some, hoping maybe it would shake the hook loose and get off. Suddenly up comes a pretty good fish—about a pound or so—and grabbed it. And there, right on its tail, was a bigger one that swallowed that one half down in one gulp. So I thought, 'Well, let's just see what happens.' You see, a fish's teeth are curved a bit and if they swallow something big enough, it's hard for them to let go. Anyhow, pretty soon I felt a tug on the rod, and sure enough I had a big one on. I had to give it a bit of line; you know how hard those trout pull on their first rush. It headed straight for the drop-off where the water goes deep and black. Suddenly the line went slack. I reeled in as fast as I could and pretty soon I could see the string of fish, but now there was another one on the end, one of those big red-sided lakers that look like spawning salmon, and are just as big. It had its teeth in the next-to-last, just behind the back fin. There must have been a foot of that fish down its throat. I picked up the net, and just as I reached over the side I'll be darned if another one just as big didn't dash up and make a pass at the head of the string. I had a second hook there that wasn't baited, just hanging out a couple of inches, and it snagged itself on that, so there it was, caught with the rest of them. Well now, you'd think I would have had quite a time landing all those fish, but actually it was easy. You see, what with all those fish each trying to swim in a different direction they couldn't go any-place at all, so I got the net under them and had them in the boat in a moment. You never heard such flapping in all your life! I weighed them when I got home, and the two biggest ones weighed seven and a half pounds each. Altogether, the seven fish weighed twenty-three and a half pounds. Quite a catch for one worm!"

At the last word, he put his finger to his chin. That's Nothing had his mouth open to speak, but he was too late. Martin Warnock took over smoothly.

"Hal, that is a good story, and I believe every word of it. It would have been easy to exaggerate a story like that and I'm glad you resisted the temptation to add a few pounds to the big trout, but that's about right for those fish in Clowhom Lake. I can't actually say that I've caught quite that many fish on one line, but I do have a story about a lot of fish, and here it is. It's not a story I tell to everyone, but I can see that you people are not a bunch of skeptics.

"There is a little creek on the shore between Narrows Arm and Jervis Inlet. It doesn't amount to much and not many people fish in it. In fact, as far as I know, no one does. But I've hunted and trapped in there and I found that there was a big black pool just where the falls come down off the hill. I always thought that pool looked good for fishing, so one day I got one of my cousins and off we went to give it a try. Being close to the salt water like that there could be some pretty big fish in there, so we took along our biggest landing net. Sure was a good thing we did, or I wouldn't be telling this story.

"We anchored the boat, took our rods and the net and rowed ashore. Jim took one look at that little creek and said, 'You're crazy. Come all the way over here to fish in that? Why, a decent fish would get sunburn in there.'

"I didn't say anything, just led the way up the side of the creek, with him complaining the whole way about wasting our time. Then we came out on the banks of that big black pool and his tune changed.

"'Well, I'll be... you might just be right after all. That sure looks like a place for fish.'

"So we baited up our lines and climbed down on the rocks to try our luck. I cast out first, and I'll be damned if half a dozen good trout didn't jump right out of the water before the bait even touched it. The same thing happened when Jim swung his hook out. There were fish jumping at it from all over. Of course, we both had one on as soon as the hook hit the water, so we pulled out two nice trout and tried again. Same thing. Now this was getting boring already. Too easy. A man likes to have to do a bit of work for his fish. And just then, watching those fish chase after the bait when it was still four feet from the water, I had a great idea. 'Jim,' I said, 'I want to try something. Get the net.'

"So he did, and I told him, 'Now you just stand on that rock there while I swing the hook over the water. When we get enough fish after it, you shove the net down in front of them and they should all swim into it.'

"Jim, he thought that was a great idea, so we went to it, and it would have worked fine if Jim hadn't been so greedy. I swung the bait around the pool a couple of times, and you should have seen the school of fish that came after it! 'Go ahead,' I said, 'net them.'

"'Not yet,' he says, 'go ahead one more time.' So I did and as they came past he shoves his net in the water and the whole school of fish swum into it, but by now there were so many of them, and they were swimming so fast that they pulled him right off that rock and into the water. And what does that damn fool do but hang onto the handle, and they pulled him halfway around the pool and right under the falls. He's yelling at the top of his lungs, and I'm shouting, 'Let go, you fool, let go the handle!' Which he finally does and comes swimming out as fast as he can go. But he's still yelling, and I can't figure out why. In a moment he gets to the rock—making good time because he's going with the current—and he climbs out as if the devil was on his tail, and then I see why he's yelling. Those fish were so hungry they'd pulled his shoelaces out, and when his shoes came off they nibbled most of the skin off his feet and ankles.

"Now Jim isn't much of a man to swear, but he sat on that rock rubbing his feet and his language was enough to make a logger blush! Just then I saw the handle of the net go by so I reached down and grabbed it. It was pretty heavy, but I gave a heave and tossed it up on the bank. Would you believe there was almost thirty pounds of trout still in it? I don't know how many there were, we never thought to count them, and I wouldn't want to guess because you might think I was stretching it. But I suppose it shouldn't really count because they weren't caught on a rod."

At the last word, he touched his chin.

During the last minute or so they had been watching their prey without seeming to do so. He was on the edge of his chair, body tense, fingers working nervously. As the story ended he rose half out of his chair, opening his mouth to blurt out his denial, but again he was too late. Wolf took over without a pause and a rigid etiquette forbade interruption. It just wasn't done if you expected to be invited another time.

"Martin," said Wolf admiringly, "that was a good story, and I'm sure it's true because who could make up something like that? The trouble is that I don't know how anyone could top it," with a sly glance at That's Nothing squirming around in his chair. "But I do have a story about a pretty big fish that is a little bit different than most and I was thinking that it might just interest you to hear it." He waited for the chorus of encouragement to swell, then fade.

"This happened on the Brem River in Toba Inlet. You know that country, Martin, don't you? Well, you remember the rapids just a half mile or so in from the salt chuck? Sure you do, but did you ever walk up the left side of the river where the solid rock is? That's the place where my story happened. I went up one day a couple of miles from the beach, and then fished down the river. Worked through all those nice pools above the rapids but didn't raise much. There were fish there all right but they just weren't biting that day. When I got to the rapids I headed down the right-hand side— going down, that is. It's the easiest going, but it's kind of hard to fish. I finally came to a likely looking pool where the water swung in against the rock and made a nice deep eddy. I thought sure there would be a fish or two in there. I let my line down right in against the rock figuring they'd be lying in the slack water in the bend. But the funny thing was, instead of the line following the current around the corner and out of the pool, it seemed to keep on going straight. I thought, 'Aha, there's an undercut there.' So I kept on letting out line. All of a sudden I felt a pull that almost tore the rod out of my hands. I thumbed the reel but the line went slack and when I reeled in there was no hook. The line looked kind of frayed at the end, like it had fouled around a rock. I tied on another hook, baited up and tried again. I knew there was something big under that rock, but I didn't guess how big!

"Down went the line under the rock, just like the first time, and sure enough it snapped tight again and I set the hook hard. But I just felt one good pull on the line when it went slack again. Now, I was using pretty heavy line—forty-pound test cuttyhunk—and I hadn't expected to break it. You know how forty-pound test will straighten out most any hook if you snag a log or something. So I had only brought along three hooks. Now I was down to one. I decided that there was a sharp rock in there somewhere—because the line at the break was frayed again just like before—and that I had better give up trying to catch whatever was in there. There was still about a half mile of water I wanted to fish. So I climbed up on the smooth rock above the pool and sat down to tie on my last hook. I hadn't been on that side before so I was looking around pretty closely. It's a strange sort of place. The granite has been worn smooth and slick by the freshets, and here and there are deep potholes where the water has cut into softer rock. Some of those holes are three or four feet across and go down ten or fifteen feet. There was one between me and the river, so I got up and went over to have a look at it. Some of them are bigger at the bottom, some at the top, but this one went straight down, the same size all the way. It was about two and a half feet across. There was water at the bottom, going around in a circle like a whirlpool, and I could see from the green light showing at one side that there was a hole through into the river that led out in the direction of the pool where I'd been fishing. 'So,' I thought, 'that's probably where my line went. I'll bet there's a fish down there.' So I got out a worm and dropped it in. Came a splash and a swirl, and I knew I had guessed right. There was a fish in there, and from all the signs it was a big one. I lay down on my belly with my head below the edge so my eyes would get used to the dim light. Pretty soon I could see right to the gravel bottom. I figured the walls at the bottom must be undercut so there would be more room, or maybe that the fish was lying with its head end in the tunnel, but no, I could see the walls right down to the bottom and no fish. So I got out another worm and dropped it in. The current caught it and swung it around close to the wall, and again there was this great swirl and splash and still I couldn't see the fish.

"And then I did. I realized that the dark circle that I had thought was a band of different coloured rock was actually the fish. It had grown so big that it went right around that little pool so that its head went about eight inches past its tail! It must have gone in there when it was small, and grew so big on all the food that the current brought in, that after a while it couldn't get out. Then of course there was no place to grow but around in a circle until its head caught up with its tail.

"Well, I just had to get that fish. I baited up and let down my line. There came that swirl and splash again. Now of course the fish couldn't go anywhere, so I didn't expect it to put up much of a fight. But that fish was used to swimming in a circle. It went round so fast that the water rose up on the sides and down in the middle so that it looked like a funnel. I figured the hook and the cuttyhunk could take the strain, so I gave a pull, but that was my mistake. When I flipped the fish over on its side, it was going so fast that it rolled halfway up to the top of the hole. Of course that twisted the line up and made knots in it so that when it fell back, the line came up tight and broke the hook. Well, there I was. So I sat there thinking for a while. Suddenly I had an idea. Can any of you guess what I did?"

"No," said Martin Warnock, "but I just know you are going to catch that fish!"

Wolf looked at him reproachfully. He said, "A more suspicious man than I am would almost think that you are skeptical about this story."

"No, no, it's not that. I believe you every bit as much as I know you believed the story I told a little while ago. No, I was thinking of that fish. There used to be lots of them like that, but they all got caught out, once people knew where to look and I was sort of hoping that you'd leave that one. So, what was your idea?"

"Well," Wolf went on, apparently somewhat mollified, "it was this. I went along the bank where the wood was that the freshets had brought down, and I found a nice straight pole about two inches on the butt and about fifteen feet long. Then I got a short stick about a foot long and tied it to the small end of the pole with the rest of my line so that it made a kind of sharp-pointed *V* shape. I lowered it down the hole until it was below the fish, and then I pulled up on it. The fish hung in the *V* and I hauled him out of that hole like you might hook up a tire with a pike pole. You see, I had figured out that he had been in that hole so long that his backbone had to have grown stiff, and he just wouldn't be able to straighten out any more. And I was right. He came up in a perfect circle and stayed that way. When I knocked him on the head and tried to straighten him out, he snapped right back into a circle again. I stepped back and looked at him. He was an ugly-looking brute, as skinny as a snake. Then I realized that if he made a circle two and a half feet across, that that fish would be about eight feet long if you straightened him out! Now that is a pretty long fish even for that river, and I was wondering how he got so long and thin when it suddenly came to me. I realized that when he got halfway round the circle he would see his own tail, and would think it was another fish. Now, by the time he grew that big, there wouldn't be enough food getting in that little hole, so he would be trying to catch that other fish all the time. Naturally that would stretch him out quite a bit. Then when he found it was his own tail he would have got into the habit of growing and it would be hard to stop."

"Now, that is a real good theory," Martin Warnock said seriously, "and I always wondered how those fish got so long."

Wolf looked at him for a moment, then continued. "Well, skinny as he was, that fish still weighed about twenty pounds, and it was real hard to carry him over the rocks all curled around like that. So I went back up a ways to where I could cross to the other side, and then I cut over to the trail. Once on the trail it was easy; I just rolled him along like a kid rolls a hoop. The trouble was it was too easy and I got careless. When I got to the long hill that goes down to the flats, he got away from me and went rolling and bouncing down that hill just like a car tire. And there, standing in the middle of the trail just before the bend, was a big black bear. He was trying to see what the strange noise was, swaying his head from side to side like they do when they don't know what's going on. But you know how bad their eyes are, he couldn't see a thing. And I'll be darned if that fish doesn't hit a rock, fly up in the air and make a dead ringer over that bear's head! It was a perfect fit, and it looked just like a horse collar around his neck!

"That was the scaredest bear I ever saw in my life. Here he was walking up the trail minding his own business when something wraps itself around his neck and won't let go. That bear started off so fast he was running for about five seconds before he started to move. Then he took off up the draw like a rocket, and just as sure as I'm sitting here, if he didn't stop he's running yet! And that's why no one but me ever saw that fish."

"Now, that," said Father quickly, "is quite a story. There are people who would hesitate to believe a story like that. Of course, I'm not one of those people. I will say, though, that there are one or two points that seem just a bit unlikely."

"Such as what, for instance?" challenged Wolf in tones of deepest injury.

"Well, for one thing, for that fish to have hit that stone just right, and for it to fit just so over the bear's head. But of course it certainly could happen, and I'm absolutely certain that you wouldn't be wrong on a thing like that. I guess, Martin, that Wolf gets the prize for the biggest fish. A trout eight feet long is pretty hard to beat."

That was too much for That's Nothing, who had been squirming restlessly on his seat for the last half-hour or so. He couldn't take it any longer. Without waiting to see if Father had finished, he came out with a "That's nothing!" that was probably quite a bit louder than he had intended. Every head turned in his direction. He looked around defiantly, his face flushed with excitement. "That's nothing," he said again firmly. "Not where we come from. Where we come from a twenty-pound trout wouldn't be worth talking about, would it, Mabel?"

"No dear."

"Now, I know a place up the coast where there are some really big fish. There was this place up in the hills no one else knew about. You see there was this creek—

not too big, you could walk across it—and it was pretty steep so no one fished it. But I knew that about a mile up, there was a flat, level spot about half a mile long where there were some real good deep pools. Once in a while when we got tired of catching little ten- or fifteen-pound trout, I would say, 'Mabel, let's go up the mountains and catch some real fish for a change.' So she'd pack a lunch and I'd get the bait ready. The best bait was meat cut up in chunks about two inches thick. I'd cut up a couple of dozen pieces, get my rigging out and away we'd go. It would take us about two hours to get there, because we had to go about ten miles by boat. Well, when we got up to where the pools were, I'd take the axe and cut me a pole about twelve or fourteen feet long—that would get me out to the deep water—and I would tie about the same length of line to the end of it. No use using a reel, those fish would just tear it apart. I always used the strongest cuttyhunk you could get, one-hundred-pound test, and the biggest cod hooks you could buy. Then I'd put on one of the chunks of meat and I was ready. I didn't use a sinker, the weight of the meat would put it down. As soon as it got near the bottom, I'd have a fish on. No use trying to play them. I'd just put the pole over my shoulder and drag them up the bank. The small ones would go thirty pounds or so, wouldn't they, Mabel?"

"Yes dear."

"Of course, every once in a while I'd hook into a really big one, and he'd snap that line just like a thread before you could give him slack. You never got a chance to land one of them. Of course, it would be too heavy to carry down the mountain anyhow. But that's what I call real fishing, and some pretty good-sized fish!"

There was a space of silence after this. Some of the people looked a bit embarrassed, as if they felt some comment was called for but couldn't bring themselves to make it. Everyone there knew that fish on the coast get smaller as you go farther up the mountain if the creek is too steep for saltwater fish to get up it.

Martin Warnock was the first to move. He stood up, walked over to That's Nothing, and, taking hold of his arm carefully, felt his bicep.

"What's the matter? What are you doing?"

"We-e-e-ll," said Martin, "I don't doubt your story; that wouldn't be polite. I just want to feel the muscle on the man that can break hundred-pound-test cuttyhunk on the end of a twelve-foot pole."

His victim squirmed and stammered, not quite knowing how to take this. Finally he managed lamely, "I guess I'm a bit stronger than I look."

"Yes, I guess so. Something like that, anyhow!"

Now, it would be nice to be able to say that Father's plan worked, and that That's Nothing became a man reformed, but I'm afraid the truth is that it had no effect at all.

Martin Warnock went back to Pender Harbour, leaving Father and Wolf to cope as best they might. It was now open season for deer, and Father brought in his first buck of the year. Almost everyone hunted in those days. Where there are no stores or refrigeration, fresh meat is more welcome than we can imagine.

There are lots of things to eat in the coast inlets: clams, oysters, cod, flounder, etc., and most of them are easy to gather or catch. But not for TN. For him the cod weren't biting, the flounders were "muddy" and the tides not right for clams or oysters. Besides, they were too small a game to be worth his while. What he wanted was deer meat, but deer were amazingly elusive for such an accomplished hunter. He not only caught no deer, but the effort to do so left him with no energy to catch anything else. If it hadn't been for his wife's vegetable garden, they would have been close to starving, for the camp boss, after calculating the results of TN's first month of employment, indicated emphatically that a second month wouldn't be required. So, aside from the occasional odd job, he had no source of income. And now, as the fall days grew shorter and the nights held the chill that heralds winter, he began to coax Father to take him hunting. He had learned somehow that Father had been a guide at one time, and from then on gave him no peace.

"It's just so I can get the lay of the land, you know. It's hard to hunt strange country. Of course, up the coast I would have had four or five deer by now, but this place is different."

Father did not want to take him hunting. He didn't even care to talk to the man. But every day, TN would find him and beg and plead with him to go on a hunt. And finally Father gave in. He told me, "I didn't do it for him. It was his wife and kids I felt sorry for. I knew they didn't have much to eat."

So the next day, off they went up the inlet, for TN

wanted to go up the river at the head. This wasn't the place Father would have chosen, but he wasn't inclined to argue once he had made his point, not least because when he expressed doubt about the idea, TN became convinced that this was the best spot and that Father was trying to keep him away from it. So they went in Father's boat as far as the river mouth, and in his canoe for the trip up the river. In the fall the river is low and it is not too hard to work a canoe up the first two rapids. From there the pools are deep and the water mostly slow-moving for the next couple of miles. The plan was to go up the river for as far as they had time, then to drift quietly down and hope to see some game on the banks and sandbars in the evening. This can be very effective in the right place. It was the method preferred by Charley "the Old Indian," friend of Father's youth, and it was often used by others of his race, but Father had walked up the river not long before, looking for grizzly, and had seen few deer tracks.

His guest crouched tensely in the bow with his gun ready. As the banks slipped by, Father reflected on what a perfect evening it was, or would have been had he more congenial company. At least the man didn't talk much, he was so intent on watching for game.

But there were no deer, and after some time of this, when they were almost back at the river mouth, TN slumped down in the bow of his canoe, his expression glum. He said, "I knew we shouldn't have come up here. This creek is too brushy. I like to hunt in the mountains where a man can see all around him."

They were just then coming down the rapids leading

into the big pool where the Hunechin Creek joins the Skwaka River. Father, always watchful, pointed. "There's your deer," he said quietly.

"Wh—where?" TN looked around wildly. He lurched to a kneeling position, thumping his gun noisily on the side of the canoe.

"There, can't you see it swimming across to that sandbar?" They were now in the pool, drifting easily about fifty or sixty feet from the deer, which was swimming strongly toward the only spot where it could climb out on that side of the pool. TN saw it. He raised his gun, then lowered it. "Closer, get closer," he whispered hoarsely.

"Closer? Why, man, if you get any closer you could club the poor thing to death."

"Closer, closer!"

Father said nothing, but held the canoe in position so they were facing the deer. TN raised the gun again. He didn't shoot, but followed the deer along with the gun as it swam steadily toward shore. Father knew what he was waiting for: the moment when the deer came out of the water so that he would have a bigger target. He said quietly, "You had better shoot if you're going to."

TN didn't answer, nor did he take the advice. The deer drew closer and closer to shore. Now it was nearly at the water's edge. Suddenly, as its feet touched bottom, it bounded right out of the water onto the sand, where two more swift bounds took it across the little beach and into the brush. TN was left kneeling there, his gun levelled, without having fired a shot. He threw the gun into the bottom of the canoe (much to Father's disgust: you do not mistreat your tools); fortunately it didn't go off. As he did so he shouted, "You crazy fool, you let it get away. What's the matter with you?"

This was the moment Father had been waiting for. He said smoothly, "Why, I was waiting to see which eye you were going to shoot it in!"

He made an enemy for life, but as he said afterwards, "I wouldn't want that kind of man as a friend anyhow."

It was a quiet trip back to camp. Not a word was spoken, but as they were going up the float, TN said in tones of great self-pity, "I don't know what we're going to do, the wife and kids haven't had meat to eat for weeks. All we have to live on are potatoes."

This was too much for Father's soft heart. He told me, "I knew there were still clams and fish of course, but just the same I went out next day and shot a nice fat spike buck and left it in front of their door. I met Mabel a couple of days later in front of the cookhouse. She came up to me and said, 'Mr. Hammond, I want to thank you for the meat. It was so kind of you! We haven't had any meat for so long.'

"'How did you know it was me?'

"'Oh,' she answered, 'no one else would do a thing like that for us.'

"I felt a little bad about that. I always felt kind of sorry for her anyhow, especially when we were all gathered together of an evening. No one ever spoke much to her. I used to wonder what she was thinking, sitting there listening to her man making a fool of himself in front of everybody. I got to watching her whenever he was telling one of his 'brags,' and I noticed something that made me think a bit. When he would ask her 'Isn't that right, Mabel?' and she would answer 'Yes dear,' a few minutes afterwards when she thought no one was looking, she would smile a secret sort of smile. I'd sure like to have known what she was thinking then!"

SILENCE

I t's almost impossible for someone of our time to understand how strange, and sometimes menacing, the coastal inlets of British Columbia seemed to the first Europeans. Unmapped, often unexplored, in many places untouched by the feet of humans since the great ice had receded. Much of it not lived in or even travelled through by the Native peoples, whose stories did little to make anyone feel more at ease in it. They never spoke freely about such things, but to someone such as Father who liked them, and—perhaps more important—treated them as equals, they would sometimes make an exception.

They spoke of valleys where one did not go, and stretches of water where one did not canoe at night. In some places there were even signs painted on the rocks to warn strangers to be careful. In fact, most of the mountains were simply not intruded on, except for special trails which had in some fashion been made safe, and on which one might travel to gather a resource, such as cedar roots—found high on certain mountains—which were much tougher and more pliable than others more easily obtained.

But when Father tried to discover just what it was that made some places unsafe, he got no satisfaction. Perhaps his innate skepticism was too noticeable, for Father's mysticism was of a different sort from theirs, and in him the mountains inspired no fears. But even he wasn't immune to the lonely savagery of the deserted inlets and valleys, and once he came near to experiencing something more. It happened like this.

The Sechelt people didn't stay in their river-mouth village at the head of Jervis Inlet in winter, preferring the much milder climate of Sechelt village. But in late spring when the berries began to ripen, they would head up the inlet in a flotilla of canoes to their age-old site at the mouth of the river. There they would pick berries, catch salmon, gather roots and herbs and, in general, have a good time.

This particular year, Father towed the canoes up to the village. He often had a few canoes behind him when he went up or down the inlet, for it's a long way to paddle, and the winds are unpredictable. Thus, although the paddlers were quite capable of going to Alaska and back if they chose to do so, being a sensible people they never missed an opportunity for a tow.

He was working a hand logging claim near the upper end of the inlet, and chancing to be in Sechelt about the time of the annual journey, let one of his friends know that he would be going back on a certain day if they wanted to hitch a ride.

When he came to his boat that morning at the Porpoise Bay wharf, they were all there before him, ready to go. There was much laughing and joking, for the Native people have a great sense of humour. They offered to race him to the head of the inlet, and immediately started off in a grand flurry of splashing and shouting.

Father loaded his boat with provisions for himself and for a small logging outfit that was halfway to the head. He caught up with the canoes about a mile up the inlet and stopped to let them tie on, then off they went, a small, green, gas boat followed by a string of about twenty canoes.

"It was an odd sort of sight, I guess," said Father, "but they pulled easily and didn't hold me back at all."

So he delivered the fleet to the head of Jervis Inlet and went about his business. June passed, and July, and still Father worked on his claim, persuading reluctant logs to slide down the hill and into the water. But one day in early August, he chanced to look out over the inlet through a gap in the trees and saw the entire flotilla of canoes heading down-inlet toward Sechelt.

"Now, I was surprised at this," he said. "They never left that early. The salmon run had barely started yet, and the best berries were just getting ripe. One or two canoes might go back and forth, but this was the whole camp moving out. I worked for a while, but pretty soon I couldn't stand it any longer. I had to go and find out what was up."

He put away his tools, went down the slope to his boat and headed out across the inlet. As he approached the canoes—all bunched up, not strung out in a line as they usually were—he cut the engine and coasted to a stop.

The canoes clustered around, and he noticed right away that the occupants weren't their usual happy and noisy selves. They looked grim, and even the children seemed subdued. Something was definitely wrong. As the largest canoe pulled alongside, Father hailed the big man sitting in the stern.

"Hiya Chief! What's the matter. Aren't you going in the wrong direction? Never thought I'd see you get lost in these waters!"

But his friend was in no mood for joking. "Huh," he grunted. "Glad you come. We want tow bad. Go faster."

Father was immediately concerned. "What's the matter? You got sick?"

The other shook his head. He seemed reluctant to speak. Finally he said, "Spirit bear come. Very bad. Must leave, not come back this year. Now we go?" His manner indicated quite clearly that further talk on that subject would be unwelcome.

While they had been talking, the other men had tied the canoes together with that speed and efficiency which they could exercise so well when they chose.

"I hadn't intended to go to Sechelt that week," said Father, "but when they wanted a tow so bad, I couldn't disappoint them, so down the inlet we went. But it wasn't until we slowed down to land at Porpoise Bay wharf that they began to talk and laugh like their old selves."

Now that he was there, he decided that he might as well stay over. If he was to turn around and head back right away, they would know that he had gone out of his way for them, and they would feel obligated. He was unusually sensitive to this sort of thing. Besides, he was curious.

He waited for an opportune moment, then singled out the man he knew best in the group, one with whom he had fished and hunted and whom he had known for years, and who spoke English better than many Europeans. They exchanged a bit of news, then Father asked casually, "Say, what's this 'spirit bear' thing all about? I never heard of anything like that before."

The other was silent so long that Father thought he wasn't going to answer. At last he said, "Hal, this is not something I can talk about. For one thing, it is about the old ways, and the priests at the school forbid it. Now, I know that you know that wouldn't really stop me from telling you. But it's also about something that I can't explain to you because there are no words in your language for it. At least, none that I know. And then, it might make me sound foolish to you, and I wouldn't like that. Now, how is the handlogging going? Is the bark still slipping?"

"I could take a hint as well as the next man," said Father. "I didn't ask any more questions."

The next day he loaded a few provisions and headed back, but instead of stopping at his claim, he kept going until he was at the mouth of the Skwaka River. There he anchored, paddled ashore, and pulled his canoe up into the grass.

"I had my 38:55 with the magazine loaded, and a pocketful of shells besides. Some of those men—and women too!—would tackle a bear with a pocket knife. If there was something in there bad enough to chase them home, I wanted to see what it was, and I wanted to be ready for it. My guess was that it might be a white grizzly. It had to be something pretty unusual and something that would be sacred somehow. Nothing normal would do it. Those men didn't scare easily."

He walked up along the bank of the river on the side the houses were on, farther along the bay. He was alert for any sign of the unusual, any sound. But at first everything seemed quite normal. The summer sun beamed warmly through the trees and flashed off the tumbling rapids.

"I didn't notice anything for a while. A man can't help being a bit jumpy in a situation like that. After all, something spooked those people. But after a while, I got just a bit of a feeling that something wasn't quite right, and then I realized what it was. Now this might sound like something out of a story book; in fact, I've read about exactly the same thing. What it was, the woods were too quiet; and it came to me suddenly, there were no squirrels. What would make a squirrel shut up? If anything bothers a squirrel, it just runs up a tree and swears at it. And I looked and there were piles of cone bits on the logs, but they were at least a week old. No fresh ones. That made me think. But I figured maybe some marten had moved in, or hawks. So I went down to the sandbar at the first big pool where the two rivers join, to look for tracks. Well, there were plenty of tracks. People, deer, coon, black bear. But they were all three or four days old. I crossed over and walked up alongside the rapids to the next pool, where there was a long sandbar. Same thing. Now you have to have lived in a place like that, and hunted there, to know how unlikely that was. It just didn't make any sense to me that all those animals had pulled out.

"And now comes the part that's most hard to tell to anyone. I stood there on that bar listening to the river. The sun was shining from a clear sky. It was two o'clock in the afternoon, and suddenly it seemed to me that the warmth was draining out of the sunshine. Standing there in the bright sun, I felt a cold shiver go down my back, and I got the feeling that something was watching me. No, that's not quite right. More like something knew I was there and didn't like it. I cocked the rifle and checked that there was a shell in the chamber: I knew there was, but I felt better checking it. Then I walked along the side of the river for about a quarter of a mile. It took me about an hour, what with stopping every few yards to look and listen. Once, a pair of sawbill ducks flew downriver as fast as they could go. That was the only sign of life I saw or heard. I got so tired of all that quiet that I raised the gun to fire a shot into the woods, but then I lowered it again, without shooting. It just seemed like it wasn't such a good idea after all.

"By now the sun was getting pretty close to the tops of the mountains, and I got to feeling that I didn't want to be in that valley when it went behind them, though it would be light for hours yet. So I struck off down the river, shoved the canoe off and paddled out to the boat. And I wouldn't want to say how many times I looked behind me! But there was nothing there, and I never did see anything in any way unusual, so I guess this really isn't much of a story.

"There's nothing more to tell. I started to make supper, but then I decided I'd enjoy it more if I was farther down the inlet, so I fired up the engine, and away I went to the claim. I never did find out what a 'Spirit Bear' was, but I'm pretty sure that I wouldn't want to meet one!"

"But," I asked him once after he had told this story, "just what do you think was in there? What chased the animals away? What could make you feel like that in a place you knew so well?" For I knew he must have thought about this many times.

"Nerves," he answered. "That's all it was. Just nerves. Being alone in there with the woods all quiet, and the river talking. You know how strange and lonely a place like that can be sometimes. And the village being deserted like it was. Just nerves."

But his voice lacked conviction.

the joke

Though Father's sense of humour sometimes landed him in hot water, at least once it was someone else's that caused the trouble.

Four hunters wanted to hunt the head of Jervis Inlet and had hired Father as their guide. They were all rather large and emphatic men who had hunted together before. They knew and used all of the "hunters'" words, such as "bag" for catch, "mowitch" instead of deer, "skookum" for big or very strong.

They were very fond of practical jokes. On each other sometimes, but especially on their guide. Father liked jokes well enough if they weren't of the cruel variety, although being the constant butt of them annoyed him. Still, he was getting well paid for the trip, so he resigned himself to the situation. Besides, he thought that once the sixty or so miles to the head of the inlet were behind them, the men's energy would go into hunting.

But the hunting didn't go well. The late fall storms had arrived, and the rain was almost frightening in its violence. The narrow valley between the sheer mountains echoed to the roar of water pouring down the rock walls. The animals stayed under cover, and the hunters were down to their last dry clothing by the second day, although they had spent most of the time in the boat.

"And let me tell you," said Father, "it is no laughing matter to be cooped up in a small boat with four practical jokers."

That evening the rain stopped, and the hunters were sitting around the stern cockpit while Father made supper. He had borne their tricks and chaffing stoically and ignored their comments on his lack of ability as a guide, but when they arranged a bucket of water to fall on him when he came out of the companionway, drenching his last dry clothes, he resolved to get even.

His idea wasn't an original one, and he didn't really expect it to have much effect. He was carrying some dynamite to deliver to a farmer up the coast, so he opened the locker and took out one stick and a bit of fuse. After undoing the end, he carefully extracted the dynamite and refilled the cylinder with sand from the box the stove sat in. He inserted a short fuse and lit it. Then he opened the door and announced, "Here's how we get fish for supper when they're not biting." He stepped over the raised door sill onto the deck, pretended to stumble and dropped the stick of "dynamite" onto the deck between the four men.

"Look out!" he yelled. "Short fuse, it's going to blow!" Then he ducked back into the cabin and watched.

Three of the hunters leaped into the water, but the fourth reacted quite differently. All his muscles went limp, and he sagged on his seat like a great jelly, moaning, "I'm done for, I can't move." Then his eyes turned up, his face went dead white and he fainted.

This was a bit more than Father had expected, but as it was his worst tormentor he wasn't very contrite. It did occur to him to hope the man didn't have a weak heart!

By now the others were calling to one another, "What happened?" "Why didn't it go off?" and then, "Come on, boys, it must have been a dud." In a

moment—with Father's help—they were back in the cockpit. The one who had fainted woke up and got shakily to his feet. Someone said, "That's the last dry clothes." The dry one looked down incredulously. He said in a strained sort of voice, "I've messed myself." He looked around. There was an uncomfortable silence. He said quietly, "If anyone of you refers to this, ever, I'll kill him!" He sounded as though he meant it.

Father thought that it might be a good idea to throw the "dynamite" overboard, but as he reached for it, one of the men put his foot on it, remarking, "There's something funny going on here." He picked it up, sniffed it, carefully pulled the fuse out. A bit of sand trickled out of the hole. He caught some in his hand. "Sand," he said. They all looked at Father.

Later he told me, "I was never looked at like that before or since. I think I know what it might be like to face a lynch mob!

"Jumping back into the cabin, he slammed the door and locked it. He ran to the bow. There was a narrow space under the foredeck where the fuel tank was. He reached it just as they kicked the door down. He snatched up a pair of caulk boots from under the bunk, crawled in the hole and got his back to the bow, where he slipped the boots on and laced them hurriedly.

"Pull him out of there," someone shouted. One of them crawled in. There was only room for one. When he was within range, Father kicked at him with the spiked boots.

There was a yell of pain and rage. "I can't get at him, he's got spikes on!" He backed out, swearing.

Someone said, "Get the pike pole." The next minute they were jabbing viciously at Father with the sharp spike and trying to gaff him with the hook, but because of the angle of the bow and the gas tank they couldn't quite reach him. They were frantic with rage and frustration.

"They were like a pack of dogs with a cornered coon," Father said. "They weren't human at all just then."

There was a pause while they changed their clothes from the soaking wet to the just damp ones hanging by the stove. They considered what to do next. That worried Father. Their first actions had been impulsive. But now they were after him in earnest.

Finally one said, "Get the axe. We'll chop a hole in the deck. Two of us in here, two on deck, we'll soon pull the bastard out of there."

"What'll we do with him?" another asked.

The one who had fainted, laughed. It wasn't a nice sound. "Get him out. I'll show you what to do with him." There was the sound of the axe being taken from its fastenings. Father called out, "I wouldn't do that if I were you, unless you want real trouble."

There was a pause; then one said, "You're bluffing."

Father opened the drain on the gas tank, and quickly closed it. "Smell that," he said. And then quietly but firmly, "No one is going to 'take me' on my own boat. At the first sound of the axe, I'm going to light a piece of my shirt soaked in gas and throw it under the floorboards. Then I'm going to go out that door, and I don't think all of you together can stop me. Even if you do, when the fire reaches the gas—in about ten seconds, I figure—you're going to have a long walk home. That is, if you make it to shore. And if you do, what will you do then? Do you know where to head across the mountains to outside? If you want to try, let's get on with it.

"Or you can agree to a truce. After all, what are you so fired up about? I thought you fellows could take a joke as well as you could dish one out. I guess I was wrong, but why blame me? You sure talked like good sports!"

There was a long silence.

"After the first ten seconds went by, I knew I'd won," Father told me. "At a time like that, if you can just get people to think, it's all over."

The most reasonable one finally spoke. He said, "You know, he's right. What the hell, we only got wet, and a scare."

"*You* only got wet," said the dry one venomously. But once they began to talk, the crisis was over. They agreed to a truce, and no more hazing—or not much anyway. And that evening, after an especially good supper, a couple of them could even get a chuckle out of it.

"That stumble sure looked real. Would you really have fired the boat, Hal?"

"I sure would have, and I'd have got back home, too. Probably would have had to give up guiding, though. Hard to explain losing four hunters!"

So it ended amicably enough. The next day was dry, and they even bagged two deer to bring back. But it was not the same party going home as heading out. There were odd silences. And at least one of the men— Father thought—would never be quite the same again.

The Deer???

The place, one of the inlets beyond Pender Harbour. I think it may have been Narrows Arm. Why they picked that particular valley, I don't know, but Father had promised to take his friend "Shorty" Roberts on a hunting trip, and this was the place they chose. Probably because neither of them had hunted there before, nor knew of anyone else that had.

They dropped anchor at a creek mouth, in a bay where the water was calm and sheltered. Though it was late in October and the weather stormy, they wouldn't have to worry about the boat.

Father looked around them as Shorty was getting into the skiff. The mountains were almost completely covered with clouds that came to only a few hundred feet above the water. There was almost an inch of snow at the beach, and the trees were more white than green. A few small snowflakes were drifting down. It would be hard, he thought to imagine a more gloomy prospect. Steep hills all around them, grey sky close above, snow.

Shorty was as excited as a hunting dog when its master takes the gun down.

"Shorty wasn't much to look at," Father said, "but he was all heart and sinew. He could walk all day with his boots full of snow and his clothes soaking wet and never seem to notice it. He never complained. He loved to hunt. I never saw a man who enjoyed hunting as much as Shorty did. He could never get enough hunting."

"What a perfect day, Hal! Just enough snow, and fresh too. Any tracks will be today's—we should have a great hunt!" He knew that Father was aware of all this, but his excitement had to have an outlet.

They rowed ashore, pulled the skiff above high tide level, and headed up the valley. It was quite steep at first, and hadn't been logged except for a few trees near the shore that had been taken out by handloggers. After a hundred yards or so, the slope became more gradual before rising into the foothills of the mountains. They kept to the left side where a considerable area had been burnt not long before. This would be the most likely place for deer, for they like to browse on the bushes that grow up in a burn and tend to avoid old-growth forest if possible, although they like to bed down on the edge of it.

They had scarcely entered into the burned area when they heard the thump of hooves. The sound was of a heavy deer, and they both spotted it at the same time, a huge buck showing for a second or two between the clumps of young trees.

"Man oh man!" breathed Shorty. "Did you see that rack of horns? There's our buck!"

In a few moments they were looking at the tracks in the snow.

Shorty was awed. "Will you look at those tracks! That deer must go over two hundred pounds. We've just got to get him. Let's go."

They checked their rifles and began to follow the tracks. As they went along, they both scanned the country around them alertly. Sometimes a deer will stand and watch you from some vantage point, curious as to what might be following it, especially in a place where they have seldom or never been hunted, such as this valley.

They walked steadily on, not making much effort to be silent, for they could never be silent enough that the deer wouldn't hear them. But suddenly there were no more tracks. They just stopped in a patch of clear ground. There was—at this height—about two inches of snow.

"He must have made a jump," said Shorty. "Let's circle."

They separated, each taking one half of a little circle around the point at which the tracks disappeared. But they found no tracks. Aroused now, they coursed the area checking for bare spots where the snow hadn't stayed, or anywhere that a track might be concealed. Nothing.

"Well," said Shorty. "I'm damned if I ever saw anything like this. What do you think, Hal?"

Now, Shorty was a good and enthusiastic hunter, with an average talent for observation, but Father was a superb tracker, by far the best I've ever known.

"I knew I hadn't missed anything," he told me, "and I was pretty sure the deer hadn't suddenly sprouted wings and flown away. There was only one thing left."

So he looked carefully at the tracks in the snow. It wasn't easy as they had walked over most of them.

"Shorty," he called. "Come here and look at this."

Shorty came to where Father was standing. "Look there. What do you think of that?"

Shorty looked at the track. Then he got down on his knees and poked at it gently with his finger. He rose to his feet. "That deer has walked backwards in his own tracks. I never even heard of a deer doing a thing like that."

"Neither have I. That must be some smart deer. Probably so old and tough you'd have to chew the gravy."

"Well," said Shorty, "let's backtrack and find where he cut off. Don't see how we missed that."

Back they went, walking slowly, looking carefully at each side of the line of tracks. After they had gone about a hundred feet, Father knelt and examined one of the tracks closely.

"We've missed it. This is a single print," he announced. "Okay, You go up, I'll go down. We'll find the spot this time."

Now they walked about fifteen feet away from the line of footprints. They had gone some fifty feet when Shorty called, "Come here, Hal."

When Father had climbed up to where he was standing, Shorty pointed. There were the tracks they had been seeking, bunched closely together behind a little clump of brush, where they couldn't be seen from where the other tracks were. Father looked around. Then he walked further uphill to where a small tree had fallen. Another set of bunched tracks was concealed behind it. They led along beside the tree, then angled off up the hillside.

He shook his head. "A deer that smart, a man could feel like a murderer shooting. But," he continued, not fully convincing even himself, "nature is a wonderful thing, and instinct is sometimes just as good—or even better—than thinking. A deer is, after all, just a deer. A wild animal."

Shorty stood there looking serious. Finally he said, "Yeah, I suppose you're right. Let's go after him."

They followed the tracks, paralleling them now, not walking on them. Suddenly, Father, who was leading the way, said, "Well I'll be darned. Look at that!"

They had come up to a bushy young fir tree about as tall as a man. The deer had gone behind it, then had turned around and faced back downhill.

"What's so funny about that?" asked Shorty. "He just turned around to see if we were coming after him."

"Look closer. He's been standing there for quite a while. I'd say for all the time we spent trying to find where he went. Just his head sticking out from behind this tree. He knew we couldn't see him, and he was curious. Those tracks are only minutes old. He started off again when he saw we had caught on to him. Not very fast either. He's not much afraid of us."

Shorty made no answer, which was strange, for he always had some comment about everything.

"Let's go," said Father. "He can't be more then a couple of hundred feet ahead of us. We should be able to spot him in this burn."

But they didn't, and as they went on, the reason became clear.

"That deer," he told me, "always managed to keep

something between him and us. It was uncanny the way he did it. I know that at any time he was never too far away for us to see him, but we never did."

And once again the tracks disappeared. Father had been expecting this to happen. He was sure the deer would try something else to throw them off the trail. They stopped where the tracks ceased and looked around them. Father knelt and examined the last few tracks.

"Nope," he announced, "he didn't backtrack this time. I didn't think he'd repeat himself. Let's start looking."

They circled the area, checking everything that could possibly conceal tracks. The ground was wet and soft, spotted with scattered outcrops of rock, most of which had no snow on them, as the ground water kept them a bit warmer. Father passed near one of them, then turned back and looked at it more closely. He beckoned to Shorty and pointed to the rock. There was a small fragment of mud and snow on it.

"He's jumping from rock to rock," Shorty said, "using them as stepping stones." He looked around. "It's going to take us a long time to find which ones he's used."

"No," said Father. "I don't think we'll have to do that."

"Why not?"

"I think that deer is standing out there not far away, watching to see how long it takes us to find his trail again. Probably just over that ridge there. If we spread out a bit and move straight toward it we should jump him and maybe get a shot at him. What do you think?"

"I don't know what to think," answered Shorty

slowly. "But I'm game to give it a try."

This didn't sound like the Shorty Roberts that Father knew. He looked sharply at his friend.

"His shoulders were all hunched up," Father said, "and there was no sparkle in his eyes. But I thought, 'He'll perk up when we spot that deer again.'"

So off they went, separating so as to approach the ridge from two different angles. Father whistled at Shorty, and pointed. There were the tracks, leading to just where he thought the deer would be. But they saw no deer. It had been there, and it had been watching them just as it had before, but once again it had slipped away as they approached, taking cover in such way that they couldn't sight it.

"He's bound to slip up if he keeps on playing tricks like this," Father said confidently.

Off they went once more, the tracks leading them on, so easy to follow. The snow was falling faster now, but they could still see far enough to shoot, if their quarry should happen to show itself. The trail led straight up the valley toward the unburned timber, and this time they walked for about fifteen minutes before the tracks came to an end.

Father knelt for a look. "Hasn't backtracked." He walked downhill a bit, looked back. Shorty was standing there, rifle under his arm, shoulders in that uncharacteristic hunch, his hat and jacket powdered with snow, looking up the valley, making no effort to find the trail. Father watched him for a moment but the puzzle was too intriguing to waste any time wondering. He cast back and forth like a hunting dog, forward and back, uphill and down. He found no trace. This time the deer did indeed seem to have "sprouted wings and flown away." He went back to where Shorty was still standing.

He said half jokingly, "Two pairs of eyes are better than one, you know."

"I think we should go home," Shorty replied. "It's too far to drag a big deer like that anyhow."

"Home?" said Father, incredulous. "Why, this is just getting interesting. What's the matter with you? How can you even think of going back without finding out what that deer has done this time to throw us off?"

"Hal," said his friend, more serious than Father could remember ever hearing him. "Have you ever heard of 'The-deer-that-is-not-a-deer'?"

"No, can't say as I have. How in heck can a deer be not a deer at the same time?"

"I just thought you might have. You know a lot of Indians. One of the old ones told me once," he went on, speaking very quietly, "that in some of the wild places like this valley, if a man is foolish enough to hunt there, he may meet the 'deer-that-is-not-a-deer.' It will lure him farther and farther into the mountains. If he keeps on after it, he's never seen again. You see, it's something more than a deer. And this thing we're following sure as hell doesn't act like any deer I've hunted. It thinks like a man. It knows how we hunt, what we look for. How could a deer know that? And what good would these tricks be against scent hunters, a wolf or a cougar? It's not natural. Let's go back while we can go back."

Father thought for a moment. "Well, if you ask me, your critter is going to a lot of trouble to lose us if he wants us to follow it. A nice plain set of tracks would make more sense."

But Shorty had an answer to that. "If we'd had a nice plain set of tracks, we'd have given up and be heading back to the boat by now." He pointed up to the snow-covered trees dimly visible through the snow. "Would you follow a straight-line set of tracks up into that? Course you wouldn't. If you hadn't got a shot in by the time we got in there, you'd have turned around and gone home. But as it is now, you're hooked. You can't wait to find out what that thing did this time, and what it's going to do next. That's right, isn't it?"

"I looked around," Father told me. "Everything was white or grey or dark green. The only sound was the hissing of the snow. You couldn't see more than a couple of hundred feet. I didn't believe a word of what Shorty said, but I thought suddenly of how the nearest other human was about thirty miles away by boat, how we might be the only people to ever walk into that valley, and in spite of myself, I felt something like a little cold shiver go through me. I had the feeling that we were at the end of the world, and there was no one else."

"Well Shorty," he said, "You know where the boat is. Go back there and wait for me. If I'm not back by dark, don't wait any longer. Something may come looking for you!"

He turned around and scanned the ground intently, trying to think of a way the deer could hide its tracks.

"I noticed a little clump of salmonberry bush about

two feet high," he told me, "and I thought, 'that bush should have more snow on it than that.' So I went for a look, and sure enough, there were the tracks right in the centre of the clump. I looked back at Shorty, and I thought, 'By Gad, if I was a superstitious man, I could believe there was something in his story at that.' That deer had covered about twenty feet in a single jump and landed so as to have hardly disturbed that clump of brush. It was marvellous!"

Now that he knew the way the deer had gone, he looked around to see where it could have gone next, and spotted a similar clump of browsed-down bushes about the same distance down the slope. When he reached it, there were the tracks in the middle of it. The only cover from there was a brush-covered little creek, but the snow was undisturbed on the bushes lining the bank. He walked slowly up and down examining every possible place where the tracks could be concealed, and finally he found them. They were just over the edge of where the bank sloped sharply down to the stream bed, out of sight unless you walked right along the bank. The deer must have gone into the brush here, even though the snow appeared undisturbed. He saw some odd marks on the ground.

"Shorty," he called. "Come down here and take a look at this."

All this time Shorty had stood unmoving where the tracks had ended. Now he climbed down to where Father was.

"What do you make of that?" Father asked, pointing to the marks.

Shorty looked closely at the ground and then at the bushes.

"That deer got down on its knees and crawled under those bushes, and it didn't hardly knock off any snow doing it, in spite of carrying a rack of horns about a yard wide. Hal, do you still think that's just a deer you're following?"

"Yes, I do. A smart deer, the smartest deer I've ever hunted, but just a deer, and I'm going after him."

Shorty shook his head slowly. "I'll go along with you for a while, but I must be crazy to do it."

They pushed through to the little stream. There, the tracks disappeared again. "See there, Shorty. He's not so smart. That's the oldest trick in the book."

"Yeah, an old trick for a man," Shorty answered morosely. "Deer don't hide their trail in the water."

Father didn't answer this. He had to decide whether to try upstream or down. He headed up on the theory that the deer would head for the cover of the standing timber. He had guessed correctly. Just when they were beginning to wonder if they had chosen wrongly, there were the tracks showing clearly where the deer went up the bank.

"That's strange," Father puzzled. "He could have made it a lot harder for us here if he'd wanted to."

"He wants to keep us interested, not to make us give up and go back," countered Shorty ominously.

Now the trail led straight toward the trees, just as Father had expected. Animals don't care much for snow falling on them and will take shelter if they can. But still the deer took advantage of every little tree, every clump of brush to avoid being seen.

They reached the timber at last, and the land rose more steeply. The trail led directly uphill, and there was less chance of seeing their quarry. Still they pressed on, caught up in that obsessive excitement of the hunting animal that is part of our genetic heritage, and which those who have never felt it can never understand, although they too carry it within them.

But the chase looked hopeless now. If the deer could elude them in the open burn, there was no chance at all of them seeing it here unless it chose to let them.

Father knew this, but he also knew that animals— just like humans—grow careless when they feel that they are safe, and he was determined to keep trying for a while yet.

The land levelled out into a bench, an area of flattish ground a couple of hundred yards wide. A fair-sized creek ran through it diagonally before turning abruptly to flow into the valley—fair-sized that is, in the context of the surroundings. It was about a foot deep, three feet across, the water that deep brown colour of coast forest streamlets. The tracks led to it; they didn't continue on the other side. The two hunters stopped, looked around.

"The wading trick won't work here," Father said, "the ground is too level. Up or down?"

"You pick," said Shorty, obviously uneasy again.

"Up it is, then."

Off they went, one on each side of the stream and about ten feet away from it. They had scarcely gone a hundred feet when they came to a rock face down which the water slid noisily. They looked up. It was almost forty feet of sheer vertical rock, green with moss, with a few ferns growing in the cracks. A mountain climber would have had a hard time scaling it.

"If he got over that, I'm not going to try following him," joked Father.

They scouted around for signs, found none, and headed back down, this time a bit further from the water in case they had missed something. On they went, past the place where the tracks had led, until their way was blocked by a huge fallen fir tree lying directly across the stream. It was head high, covered with a dense growth of young trees rooted in the rotting bark. These in turn were covered with a layer of unbroken snow. Branches and debris had collected in front of the tree where the swirling, partially blocked water had collected in a deep pool of coffee-coloured water half covered by several inches of thick yellow foam. There were no tracks anywhere, save those they had followed. Again, Father coursed the ground like a baffled hound. Back to the rock face, down again on the other side to the big log, then back up to where Shorty was standing watching him. As he came near, his friend said in a voice made hoarse with emotion:

"Hal, that's it. I'm finished. If you go on from here, you go alone. For God's sake man, wake up! Surely you don't still think that's a deer standing out there waiting for us?"

Father looked at him but made no answer. He walked over to the fallen tree, then along it to the great upturned root. He went around behind it, back to the stream. He watched the dark water welling up from under the obstruction, then started across, intending to walk right around the tree. He tried once more to imagine what he would have done. Then he saw the answer, for the tracks of the deer showed plainly in the snow a few yards downstream of him, where it had walked out of the water after swimming under the tree through that black and treacherous pool, and surfacing up on the other side. A feat so improbable that it hadn't occurred to him. He looked up, feeling a sudden intuition, and there was the deer, no more than a hundred feet away, standing in full view in an open space between the trees. It was side on, its head turned toward him, looking at him, its body darkly wet, its huge rack of horns shining golden against the snow.

For a long moment their eyes locked. An animal always knows when you see it and runs off as soon as your eyes focus on it. But not this one. Then Father remembered what he was there for. He swung his gun swiftly to his shoulder, aligning the sights onto that spot by the ear that would bring instant death, as he had done so many times before.

But this time, something stayed his hand. He could feel the deer's eyes riveted on him. He thought about the chase it had led them, the calm intelligence it had shown. And then in a way it never had before, the wildness and beauty of the great animal so at home here in the snow and trees hit a soft spot that he hadn't known he possessed, and he lowered the gun without firing.

"And then," he told me, "the strangest thing happened. I had a sort of vision of an open space under the trees. There wasn't any snow. Against the dark ground was a pile of bones shining white and bare. Human bones. There were skulls lying scattered about. It must have been spring. The leaves were bright green. It was just a flash, a quick glimpse, that passed as quick as an eye blink. But when I looked up, the deer was gone."

He went back around the root. Shorty was standing near the pool.

"It dove under the log," Father said to him, "and came up on the other side. I almost got a shot at it."

"You mean it turned into a fish. Nothing else could get under that log. Look at it!" He pointed to the pool. "I'm going back now. Are you coming?"

"Shorty was scared," Father told me. "I had never seen Shorty scared before. A wounded grizzly bear wouldn't have scared Shorty. I got that end-of-the-world feeling again, and I thought of that picture of the pile of bleached bones lying under the trees. I thought of that big deer out there, waiting for us to follow him. What would he do next? I thought of what nerve it took to go into that dark pool of water carrying those horns, not knowing if you could make it through or not. I thought, 'Why did he do it?' He didn't have to. He could have made fools of us on that mountain, in those trees. He wasn't scared of us, or why would he stop and watch us? I asked myself these questions, but I had no answers.

"I said, 'Come on Shorty. It's getting late. Let's go home.'"

ThE AMBUSH

"You remember the story of how Shorty Roberts and I followed that deer up onto the mountain? And how I got to thinking of my bones bleaching up there in the weather, no one knowing where we were or what had happened? Well, it almost did happen one time, and they would have been pretty well scattered, I think.

"It was getting toward the end of the hunting season. I was coming down Jervis Inlet from the camp. The weather was fine, and I got to thinking that it wouldn't be a bad idea to stop for a hunt. So as I cruised along, I kept an eye out for a likely looking spot, and pretty soon I saw just what I was looking for. There was a nice little draw going up into the mountains, and a bit farther on there was another one almost its twin. I saw that I could go up one, cross over and come down the other one. It was pretty steep, but didn't look as though it would be too hard to cross over the hump between them and get back to the boat. If I got a deer it would be an easy downhill drag to the beach. So I ran out the anchor, put a shoreline on a tree and away I went."

Father loved to explore, to go where he hadn't been before. Hunting was often just an excuse to see new country. This day was certainly one of those times. He had no need to climb a mountain to get deer. There were plenty of those to be had on much easier ground, and closer to home.

He climbed up beside the little creek that runs down every mountain valley, however small. No matter how similar they seem from a distance, they are always different and always interesting, if your mind inclines that way.

He saw lots of fresh tracks as he went along, but there was quite a bit of undergrowth and he never managed to get a look at a deer. The trees became sparse, and the ground more steep and rocky. It was time to cross over into the next valley.

He had spent more time than he should have and he knew that it would be wiser to go back down to the boat over familiar ground, but that was just what he didn't want to do. He decided to chance it. Up and over the ridge he went, down into the upper reaches of an almost identical valley. Here though, he felt he had more chance of getting a deer, for what wind there was, blew up the hill toward him. He was hunting now, moving slowly, alertly. But this takes time, and the afternoon was waning.

Then he came to a difficult spot. Here the creek

streamed over a fifty foot drop, and the rocks were slick with moss and unclimbable. It took him almost an hour to pick his way up, across and down, with several false starts. Far below, the water of the inlet shone grey in the afternoon light. The sun had gone behind the mountains, for there is not much afternoon in those steep valleys in late fall.

He considered what to do. He would have liked to cross back over to the other valley. He knew the ground and would have no trouble going down it in the dark. But the ridge was steep here and might prove difficult. He didn't care for the thought of being halfway down the other side when night came. He could go farther down the valley he was in, to where the trees grew more thickly, make a fire and bed down for the night. But it was long since he had eaten, and the prospect of hot food and a warm bunk on his boat was hard to put out of his mind. He recalled that the lower part of the dividing ridge was timbered and hadn't seemed to be a difficult climb. There was sure to be a deer trail leading from one valley to the next. He decided to try it. As he got nearer the water he began to angle up onto the ridge. It was now dusk, and in the shadows it was becoming too dark to see small objects.

"Several times I almost stopped and built a fire," he said, "but each time the thought of that pot of hot stew on the stove drew me to it like a magnet. A man has to be crazy to do a thing like that, climbing over the rocks on a strange mountain in the dark. But then, being young is much like being crazy!"

So he kept going, and he got lucky. At least that's the

way he put it. But I think that at a high enough level, skill can seem like good luck. At any rate, he found a distinct deer trail leading in the right direction. And just in time. Once started, full dark comes very quickly in the mountains. In a few more minutes he could see only a few feet in front of him.

"But," he said, "you don't need to see very much to follow a good deer trail. It takes the natural course and you can feel your way along it with your feet." (Well, some people might, and if anyone could, it was him.) "And," he said, "it was a good trail. Must have connected more than just those two valleys. Anyway, I was making pretty good time considering the circumstances. It wasn't completely dark. There were a few stars showing between the clouds, but there was no moon. You could tell a branch was there just before it hit you in the face.

"I'd reached the top of the ridge. There was a bit of flat ground, fairly clear of brush, but there were a lot of boulders scattered about, some of them the size of a small house. The trail led around and between them. It was an eerie sort of a place, and something about it began to get to me. In those days the woods were like home to me, but it didn't feel like home there.

"Two or three times in as many minutes, I stopped and listened. There wasn't a sound. I took in a deep breath. There was something about the air I didn't like. I took a few more steps. There still wasn't a sound, but I knew I wasn't alone. I jacked a shell into the gun and swung around. I smelled a rank smell and something loomed up over me, and I fired point-blank from the hip. The muzzle flash lit up a huge black shape reaching for me. Then, of course, I couldn't see much of anything for a few seconds. I jumped back and tripped over a blueberry bush while trying to get another shell into the chamber. Something grunted and fell heavily to the ground, making quite a bit of noise. By that time I had my back to a boulder and another round ready. I stayed still as death. There was a light air blowing across in front of me, so I knew whatever was out there couldn't scent me. I heard a few scuffling sounds and the occasional moan. I had a few matches. What I would have given for a fire! But the thing might just be waiting to see where I was, and anyway, starting a fire in the dark with nothing around but blueberry brush and hemlock, when it has been raining steadily for days, was something I wouldn't even try. Especially with some big creature I might have only wounded just a few feet away. And, it could have relatives nearby.

"So I just sat there. All night. Listening. Thinking of all the stories I'd heard since I was a kid about the monsters that live in the mountains. I don't think a night was ever that long before or since. The moans stopped after a while. I didn't know whether it had died, or recovered and was watching me, and I wasn't about to go over there and find out. A match is a poor thing to shoot by.

"I sat there for twelve hours, I figure, with the gun in front of me and my finger on the trigger, and all that time I imagined I heard noises all around me, of things sneaking up on me. It's wonderful what the imagination can do with the sound a mouse makes scuffling around in the leaves. I'll never forget that night!

"Daylight came, finally. I had just about given up on it. Never was that first faint light so welcome. The birds tell you first; you know how you hear a little chirp or two? Pretty soon you realize it isn't quite as dark as it was.

"When I could see about ten feet, I got up and stretched. Then I walked carefully over to where I figured the thing was. I don't know what I expected to see. Maybe one of those big hairy people the Indians say live in the mountains. Certainly that's what I should say it was to make a good story out of it. But I'm afraid it wasn't. I never did come across one of those, though I believe the Indians are telling the truth about them. But what it was was strange enough, though I didn't realize it at first.

"What I saw was just a big black bear lying dead on the trail. I'd been perfectly safe. My shot had broken its back. I was puzzled. Black bears don't go around hunting people. It was in good shape. Not fat, but good, shiny fur. Its eyes were closed, which was odd. Then I saw that they weren't closed. It had no eyes! At least if they were there, they were covered with a thick layer of unbroken skin. It had been born blind. How had it lived? Of course bears don't have very good sight at the best of times, but it's not as bad as some people make out. It was light enough now to see, and I walked around a bit. I saw bones. Deer bones mostly, but there was part of a bear skull. No human bones that I could see, though I'd almost left mine there. I found his den between two boulders half buried in the hillside. He

had lived there for quite a while catching what came by, whatever it was—never knowing night from day. It gave me the shivers thinking of that thing waiting there listening to me coming along, and sneaking up behind me in the dark. It must have known every rock, every twig and bush on the whole flat. I often wonder how it learned what it knew. How to be silent. How it could be so silent! A deer can just about hear grass growing. How could it catch a deer? But there were a lot of deer bones. Makes you wonder, doesn't it?"

He skinned out the head and brought it back and tanned it. I can remember seeing it when I was very young. That it had no eyes didn't impress me much at that time. My mother didn't like it. When I was old enough to be interested, it had been thrown out, or lost.

MURDER AND
THE CAT KILLERS

Murder the cat was owned by—or, more accurately, owned—a wizened little old Scotsman who may have been named MacPherson. Or he may not have. Most just knew him as Mac.

Mac had been an engineer of some sort, and in that capacity had travelled the world around. Long since retired, he existed on an inadequate pension in a little cottage near Sechelt. His savings he had invested unwisely with someone he had trusted too much. He had never stopped travelling long enough to get married; he lived alone. Most people avoided him. He was known as a dour old Celt who could tear strips off your self-esteem with a few strokes of his tongue.

Father liked him. He would tell fascinating stories of the world and its foibles when he was in the mood, and in turn seemed to enjoy having an appreciative listener as he sipped at a glass of whiskey and spun his tales of far places. It is certain that Father was the only one who cared to visit the old Scot.

Indeed, he would have been a lonely man had it not been for the company of his cat, which he had rescued and adopted when it was a small black kitten. Father maintained that it was the most impressive specimen of its race he had ever seen. Long-legged, superbly muscled, it weighed over twenty pounds. It was jet black, not a white hair on it anywhere. Even its whiskers were black, and its glowing golden eyes shone with almost human intelligence. Mac called him Murder. He claimed that there was no dog in the country around, no matter its size, that didn't make a wide detour to avoid a second encounter with Murder.

Now, Murder was a cat with pride. He took it as his responsibility to help keep Mac's larder well stocked. This is standard cat behaviour. Most people who live with a cat that hunts have been presented with a mouse, rat or bird for their use if need be.

Murder, however, disdained such small game entirely, although I suppose he would snap up a mouse as soon as not. No, though I regret to have to say it, the truth must be told: Murder was a chicken thief.

He knew the location of every chicken coop for miles around, and there were a lot of them. In those days most country people kept a few chickens for eggs and Sunday dinners. And more than once one of them maintained to a skeptical audience that he had encountered a huge black cat trotting down the trail carrying a chicken by the neck, with the bird's body slung over his shoulder.

But chickens are notorious for disappearing, and so adroit was Murder at these raids that he was never caught in the act, and he was so discreet that he never visited the same place without quite some time intervening. Mac, on his part, was not loath to accept his friend's offerings in the spirit in which they were meant. The meat was a welcome addition to his frugal fare, and he felt no impulse to inquire as to its source.

"And once," he told Father, "there was a bluidy great duck at the door in the morn. I don't ken how the wee laddie carried it. The nearest ducks be at least a mile awa'."

Most of Mac's neighbours didn't realize that a mere cat was raiding their chicken pens, and wouldn't have believed it if someone had suggested it. Thus Murder's reputation was not as bad as it might have been had the truth been known. However, there was one exception.

This was a man whom I will call Tibble, as that was not his name, but gives a similar impression. Tibble owned the land adjoining Mac's cottage. He also owned some fine pure-bred chickens of which he was excessively proud, and his wife owned a fluffy white Persian cat, whose bloodlines were a matter of record for many generations. It is fair ground for speculation which infuriated Tibble more; the sight of a trail of chicken feathers leading into the woods, or the black and white kittens.

Tibble built new pens. The chickens got out, or Murder got in. His wife secluded the white Persian when she began to yowl at the moon. She got out, or Murder got in.

Tibble raged. Tibble threatened. Tibble took Mac to court, seeking an injunction that would force Mac to keep his cat home. Tibble lost.

The judge quoted an ancient law, to the effect that "A man can be said to own a dog, and thus be held responsible for the dog's actions. However, no man can be said to own a cat, thus no man can be held responsible for the actions of a cat. Case dismissed!" (In those days, the law often made sense, which may be partly responsible for the saying "the good old days.")

Tibble accosted Father, being aware of his reputation as a hunter and trapper. "Hal, I'll give you fifty dollars if you'll trap that cat for me."

Father suggested that possibly an owl or a raccoon might have stolen the chickens. At any rate, he was not about to trap Mac's cat. Tibble shouted angrily, "I've seen that black devil skulking around my place. Behind my chicken pen. I'd shoot the brute, but he's too smart."

Father was about to suggest that a man ought to be smarter than a cat, but thought better of it. Tibble renewed his offer, an immense sum for those days, but Father would have none of it. Tibble stamped off, muttering dire threats against cats.

Father and Mac had a good chuckle over the attempt and thought no more about it.

At this time he was helping build a house not far from Mac's property. His way to and from work led him past Tibble's place twice each day. On one of those trips he met the man himself on the trail. There were two dogs with him. Tibble stopped him.

"What do you think of these, Hal?" he exulted, literally rubbing his hands together. "They've never lost a cat yet. They cost me a bundle, but they're going to be worth it. Their names are Gripper, that's this one, and Grabber, over there. They're all right around kids or people, but they're death on cats," he crowed happily.

"They were quite the dogs," Father used to say, "some kind of terrier cross, big heads and shoulders and all business. I never saw two dogs work together like that. They seemed to know what each other was thinking. They were always hunting. While one checked a clump of bushes, the other one would be waiting to jump on what ran out. Incredible teamwork."

Father made some sort of reply, and got away as quickly as he could. He went straight to Mac's place.

"Mac, Tibble is out to get Murder. Have you seen his new dogs?"

"Aye, laddie," replied the old Scot. "Have nae fear. There's only twa o' them." He smiled grimly. "Murder will have them for breakfast."

"I'm not so sure," Father replied, "They work as a team. I don't like the look of them."

"Ah, weel. There's not much I can do about it, laddie."

Of course, he was right. There could be no keeping Murder in the yard if he didn't choose to stay there. But he proved wiser than they expected. He didn't like the look of those two dogs either. Although Tibble made every effort to introduce Murder to the cat killers, when he appeared with them, Murder was nowhere to be seen.

Now, it was Mac's custom to go for a walk along the beach at the same time every morning, a fact of which Tibble was well aware. On these occasions Murder stayed home. He was not the sort of cat that went for walks. Perhaps he chose to guard the house. Thus when Father, on his way to work, heard barking coming from that direction, he thought that Mac might be gone, and hurried down the short side trail that led to Mac's cottage.

Suddenly the barking changed. It became strangely rhythmic, measured, somehow ominous. Something was wrong; he began to trot quickly along the trail. He knew the feeling was justified when he came within sight of Mac's house. The gate was open. Tibble was in the yard, and the rhythmic barking was coming from underneath the house. Murder was cornered!

Father hurried through the gate. Tibble started talking, stuttering in his excitement. "Th-th-the gate was open. Th-th-the dogs have that cat cornered." Tibble's face was an odd sight. One moment he would be grinning ear to ear, then he would remember to look properly concerned and the grin would disappear for a moment, only to return even wider as he forgot to dissemble. He bent over, hands on hips, looking under the house. "Here, Gripper, Heel Grabber, heel I say." His voice lacked all conviction. He was observing the formalities for form's sake.

Father ignored him. He crouched to look into the space beneath the house. There was about three feet of room between floor and ground, but as the ground sloped up toward the back, the floor there was held by a small log, leaving not much more than a foot of space. It took a moment or so for his eyes to adapt to the dim light under the house. But when they did, there was Murder, crouched against the log, with a dog on either side of him.

"His face was enough to scare a man," Father said. "His mouth was open so far you could have put your fist in it. He never made a sound, but every time those dogs barked he jerked his head first to one side, then the other. You see, those dogs had a system, and it was just about foolproof. They would bark at exactly the same time. Each time they barked, they would hitch themselves a few inches closer to the cat. It was uncanny. Bark! hitch. Bark! hitch. Like machines.

"They were only a foot away from him now, and he knew! He knew they had him. If he went for one, the other would get him. I guess he should have tried before. Anything would have been better than letting them get that close. I think that bark had him sort of hypnotized."

Suddenly Murder moved. He flung himself on one of the dogs. But he wasn't in a good position, and perhaps the loose earth betrayed him. Anyhow, as soon as he turned away, the dog on that side pounced, and sank its teeth into the loose skin on one hind leg. When Murder snapped back to attack it, the other dog seized him by the shoulder. He was caught. He couldn't reach his attackers with teeth or claws.

And now the dogs started on the second part of their system. It too was a masterpiece of strategy. With their jaws clenched, they could still manage a muffled bark. Again it was bark! hitch, bark! hitch, only this time with every bark, they pushed away from each other with the powerful muscles of their front legs and shoulders. Murder resisted, but it was hopeless. A cat has great power to push, but not so much to pull when he can't use his legs. Also, cats tire quickly. Murder was doomed!

Relentlessly, they stretched him, longer, longer... Father didn't know what to do. There was no room to get in there. He knew that even if he could, nothing would make those dogs let go. Tibble echoed his thoughts. "Nothing anyone can do," he exulted. "Can't get room to tip them off their feet. Nothing in the world will make them loose their grip once they get it."

Father saw that Murder's spine must snap in a few more seconds. He started to duck under the house to see what he could do. He couldn't let Mac's cat be killed right there in front of him without trying something!

But suddenly there was Mac himself, his voice harsh with anger, on his knees, peering under the house. "Wha's gang—" he rasped. "They've got—" He saw.

"Murder," he yelled, "Hang on laddie, I'm comin'!"

I like to think that the sound of Mac's voice gave the cat the strength to hold on for those few seconds. Certain it is that for a few barks there was no gain as the desperate cat expended his last strength to hold his spine together. Mac threw himself under the house on his belly, wriggling with eel-like motions to the battle site. Father and Tibble couldn't think what he intended, nor see what he did. His hands were stretched before him, his back touched the floor above.

"Then there came the strangest sound I ever heard," Father said. "I had never heard a dog scream before."

Even more strange, the impossible happened. For one fatal moment, Gripper lost his grip!

Only if you know dogs can you begin to understand how unlikely this was. These breeds never let go. They can be beaten, drenched with hoses, their noses pinched, their ears crushed. They do not let go. People have tried pepper, fire, gasoline, turpentine. Nothing short of death will make that sort of dog loosen its grip. But this one did!

As Mac scuttled back out of the way, Murder, released, recoiled like a giant black spring, twisting as he went. Grabber still had him by the hind leg. The dog scarcely knew what hit him. One moment he was doing what he did best, namely, ridding the world of another cat. The next, his head was being shredded. Razor-sharp claws were raking at his lips, and a set of merciless fangs was buried in his nose, with the obvious intention of tearing it off his face. But worse still must have been the knowledge that his partner—an extension of himself—had betrayed him! The claws found an eye. His nerve broke. He released his hold and fled.

All this took about one second. The action was faster than the human eye could follow. Father was only sure of what had happened later, when he examined the dog's wounds.

A second was all it took for Gripper to recover and spring in to help his partner. Too late! Murder flung himself at the dog with an appalling ferocity that Gripper had never met with in any previous encounter with anything. It was an attack meant to inflict the greatest possible damage in the shortest time. Murder's widespread front paws flashed by the snapping teeth to find a solid grip just above and to the side of the eyes. At almost the same moment his powerful hind legs bracketed the hapless dog's muzzle, raking the sensitive lips from nose to ears. Once, twice, three times at least, shredding lips, cheeks and neck in a blur of savage punishment. It was over almost before the watchers knew what was happening.

Gripper was probably big enough to handle any cat if his nerve had held, but with slashing claws threatening to tear his eyes out, his face, lips and throat in bloody shreds, and his partner fled, Gripper panicked. Flinging Murder off him with a frantic shake of his muscled neck and shoulders (at the same time tearing one eyebrow half off), he turned and fled to a position of presumed safety between Tibble's legs.

Murder shot straight out and up the sheer side of the house as if it was a ladder, his claws leaving a distinct trail up the painted cedar siding. The deep tears in his hip and shoulders seemed not to hinder him in the least. He crouched on the roof edge, growling malevolently, eyes blazing. Across the yard was his favourite tree, with a large horizontal branch on which he liked to stretch his length. Between him and the tree were Tibble and his dogs. Tibble stooped a bit to examine the dogs' bleeding heads. Without a sound to warn them, Murder sprang.

Twenty pounds of cat landed squarely between the man's shoulders, which the big cat then used to launch himself halfway to his tree, setting all his claws deeply as he did so. Another bound and he was up the tree and onto his limb, where he sat glaring, switching his tail like a pendulum.

Tibble, though a big man, was quite unprepared for the impact. He stumbled forward, stepping heavily on Gripper's foot as he did so. Then, attempting to catch his balance, he brought his other foot forward, whereupon Gripper, having turned to get out of the way, was kicked violently in the stomach.

One has to sympathize with the poor dog. The events of the last few minutes had been beyond his worst nightmares—if he had any—of cat revenge. His eyes were swollen almost shut. One eyebrow hung down over his cheek. His lips were in ribbons. He had been humiliated. Now his master had stepped on him and kicked him. To his stunned mind there seemed to be only one thing to do and he did it. He bit Tibble on the leg! Tibble yelled, and started to curse his dog.

Mac's voice cut in, cold and clear. He was standing

in the doorway. In his hands was the biggest double-barrelled shotgun in common use, a ten gauge with a bore big enough to stick your thumb in. It was pointed directly at Tibble. Mac's eyes were chips of blue ice.

"Mon," he said slowly. "I didna leave the gate open. Ye hae hurt ma puir wee bairn. At the count of three I mean to fire a charge of buckshot aobuot four feet over ye're shoe soles. I dinna care, d'ye ken, if ye be standing in them or no."

"Now look here..." Tibble started to bluster.

"One."

Tibble looked startled, his florid face turned pale. "Come on, Hal, the man's crazy. Let's get out of here." He started toward the gate.

"Two."

Tibble walked faster. Then his nerves gave and he broke into an undignified run. Gripper led the way. Grabber followed.

Father turned toward Mac, who had lowered the gun. "Would you really have shot him?"

"Without a doubt, laddie, without a doubt." He paused. "That is, if I'd had time to find ma shells." He broke the gun. The chambers were empty.

Father laughed. "He won't be back here for a while, or his dogs either." They both grinned. Then Father thought of something. "Mac, what in the world did you do to make that dog let go? I didn't think it was possible."

Mac smiled an evil smile. "Aweel," he said, in a satisfied way, "it's worked for me on human brutes, and I kenned it would work as well on the other kind.

Just squeeze, pull and twist, laddie. Just squeeze, pull and twist!"

Murder recovered quickly from his wounds. They were in the loose skin, not the muscle. Tibble's dogs were not as fortunate. The slashes and punctures healed well enough with the aid of a few stitches, though Grabber lost the use of one eye. Their minds, however, never recovered. They never again trusted one another, nor were they ever known to kill another cat. This made Murder something of a celebrity for a while, as several pet cats had disappeared from the area since Tibble had brought in his "killers."

Tibble never again resorted to anything but threats when his chickens disappeared. One more thing: there were a lot of large part-Persian kittens in various combinations of black and white given away in that neighbourhood.

BLACK MAGIC

One of Father's early jobs was as a boom man for a small camp on—I think—Lasqueti Island. The camp was owned and operated by a man whose name—vague to my memory—may have been something like O'Brien. I will call him that. One of a type, a husky, red-faced individual, harassed by log prices, debt, bad terrain, all the irritations and worries that are inherent yet in small logging operations.

He owned or was paying for a fairly new yarding machine—steam, of course, which was quite powerful for its day, c. 1919. The operation was ground yarding, the most simple machine logging method: a small line run through a pulley or "block" pulled out the heavy mainline, which dragged the logs along the ground to a place from which they could be taken to the water.

This machine was presided over by a man whose first name was Jack. As he was—in Father's words—

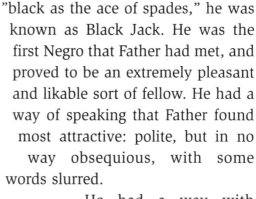

"black as the ace of spades," he was known as Black Jack. He was the first Negro that Father had met, and proved to be an extremely pleasant and likable sort of fellow. He had a way of speaking that Father found most attractive: polite, but in no way obsequious, with some words slurred.

He had a way with machinery. Those who knew him said that if Black Jack couldn't make it run, no one could.

As there weren't enough logs to keep Father working on the water all day, he took to spending time around the yarding machine, cutting wood and helping out where he could, for in this camp the engineer was also the mechanic, the fireman and the woodcutter. He was expected to do any other chore that might come up, such as hooking and unhooking the line when the logs were brought in.

The operation was in some quite good timber, on a long piece of flat ground, or "bench," some way from the water. The logs had to be moved twice: once from where they were felled to where the machine was, and from there to the water by means of a log "chute" or skidway. A third time would have raised the cost of getting them beyond the point O'Brien would have found profitable. Hence, instead of moving the machine so that the logs were brought to the chute in two or even more operations, as was usual, O'Brien relied on the power of his machine and the addition of extra line to make it in one. Half a mile, three thousand feet, thirty-five hundred, and still out, far beyond the rated capacity of his equipment. Still Black Jack somehow found enough power in his machine to move the logs. But it took more time. And the line reached out to four thousand feet.

Black Jack had long ago tied down the safety valve on the boiler. "There's no danger," he reassured Father. "The rivets will tell me when she's going to blow." This statement failed in its intended effect.

"But I was afraid he'd think I didn't trust him," said Father, "so I figured I'd better stick around."

Bringing in a log was now more than a matter of just throwing a lever. Black Jack would make sure there was a roaring fire going. He'd open the throttle until the engine screamed, then throw in the friction that engaged the gears of the big cable drum. The drum would spin wildly and the heavy cable would leap upward as it wound on. But as the line tightened, it came in more slowly until the steam pressure could no longer turn the drum. Then he would stand on the long brake pedal, get the engine racing and do it again, but this time the drum would only make a turn or two before the line stopped coming. When he had wound in every bit of line that he could in this way, he would go through the routine once more. There would be no motion of the drum, no movement in the line, which was stretched now as tight as if it were a bar of solid iron. He would then hook a wire to the handle of the brake and sit back at his ease.

"Now we'll let the steam go to work," he said, as Father watched this performance for the first time.

A steam engine, unlike one powered by gas or diesel, doesn't have to be turning continually to exert power. It will sit there still as death while the trapped, compressed steam exerts force until it cools. Depending on the design, this could take quite a while. They would sit there then, waiting. Sometimes Black Jack would take the wire off the handle, set the brake, go through the routine again. All during this time he wouldn't talk, but sit there silently, gazing intently at nothing visible to Father.

After a few minutes of this, "the wire would sort of come alive, not anything you could see directly, but if you looked out of the corner of your eye, you could see it was moving, twisting. Then it would creep, so slow you couldn't be sure you saw it, but ever faster, until at last you could see the drum begin to turn, and there would be a *chuff——chuff——chuff*, and then, chuff—chuff—chuff, and it was back to speed and the log was coming in just like normal, though he sometimes had to nurse it along a bit at first. I asked him," said Father, "just how he knew what was going on. After all, he might sit there until the steam got cold, for all I could see, but he always knew. He told me, 'Hal, it's not something you can tell. You just have to feel it in your bones.'

"This went on for a while, until one day O'Brien came striding out of the woods with a mad look riding him. A turn had just come in, and the line was going out for the next one. He came up to where we were and stood there watching. Never said a word, just stood there, thumbs hooked into his braces, elbows out. The stop signal came and we waited while they hooked on a log. The go-ahead sounded, and Black Jack went through his moves and then sat there, waiting. O'Brien says, 'What are you doing?'

"You could see Black Jack doesn't want to be bothered, but you've got to answer when the boss asks a question, so he says 'Waiting.'

"'Waiting! What are you waiting for? I've got a crew of men out there that I'm paying while you're 'waiting'. Now give her some steam and get on with it.'

"Black Jack just sits there, doesn't move a muscle, but he says, 'I'm going as fast as I can, mistah O'Brien. Have to wait till she's ready.'

"O'Brien looks at him awhile, then he says, quite quiet for him, 'That's the best you can do, is it?'

"'Yes, suh, it is.'

"'Well, we'll see about that.' And he turns and off he goes back down the trail."

A few days went by. Then one morning O'Brien came over to where Father was working on the logs. "Hal, I've got a man coming up from town on the *Cassiar*. I want you to go over and pick him up. She's due in about eight tomorrow morning."

"Who is it?" asked Father, curiously.

"A new engineer. He's factory trained, knows all there

is to know about their machines. That old layabout up there needs a lesson, and he's going to get one. He's spoilt, had it too easy. He's got a surprise coming."

O'Brien strode off with the satisfied air of a righteous man. Father finished what he was doing and went to find Black Jack, announcing indignantly, "O'Brien sent for a man to take your place!"

But his friend seemed unruffled. "It's his right to do that," he replied calmly. "Don't worry about it, Hal, it'll work out fine, you'll see." And he changed the subject with such finality that Father had no choice but to drop it.

Next morning, he was at the dock in good time. He had no difficulty in finding his man, a competent-looking sort complete with engineer's cap and toolbox.

When they got back to camp, O'Brien was there waiting for them. Impatient as always, he hustled them up the trail as soon as the new man had changed into work clothes. Father, as the youngest, carried the heavy toolbox. When they reached the machine, Black Jack was stacking wood by the firebox, waiting for the signal to go ahead.

O'Brien went up to him and said gruffly, "All right, Jack, you can haul your black arse out of here. I've got a real engineer now to get that wood moving."

The other straightened up and turned around, saying mildly, "Just as you say, mistah O'Brien. She's all ready to go. It'll sure be good to see a real engineer go to work. I think I'll just sit here awhile and watch if you don't mind. A man should never be too old to learn something."

"You can do as you please, just so you're out of the way." Then, to the new man, who was standing there looking uncomfortable, "Have you run this model before?"

"Mister," came the answer, delivered with quiet confidence, "if there's anything I don't know about this machine, believe me, it's not worth knowing!"

He walked over, got up on the sled and examined everything closely. "Looks okay."

Then he noticed the tied-down safety valve. "Who's the damn fool did this?" Without waiting for an answer, and while he was releasing the valve, he said, "You've got no warranty if you mess with this. You're lucky someone didn't get killed."

There was the hissing of released pressure as the valve functioned. Just then the whistle sounded, clear enough, but as if from very far away.

O'Brien said eagerly, "All right, there's your signal to haul her in. Let's see what you can do."

The new man gave it steam, threw in the friction, the line tightened and the machine slowed, stopped. He put the brake on, released the friction. When the engine reached its full RPM, he released brake and engaged friction with a practised, expert motion. Nothing happened, except the quick slowing of the engine. He released the brake and let the line go slack. Tried again. Same result.

He released the levers, cut the steam, turned to O'Brien. "How much line have you got out?" and, at the answer, "Four thousand feet! No wonder she bogs down. She's rated for three thousand with line this size. Level pull. She's overloaded. You'll have to move her closer."

O'Brien's face, naturally red, began to get redder. "You mean that's all you're going to do? Just sit there and tell me I've got to move?"

The engineer shrugged indifferently. "That's all anyone can do. A machine can only do so much, and that's that."

"Jesus Lord Christ!! We've been yarding wood out for a week at this distance, and now you come out here and tell me it can't be done!"

The new man shook his head. "That's what you say. I'll believe it when I see it."

O'Brien turned to where Black Jack was sitting. "All right, Jack, show him."

But Black Jack only put his hands under his hip pockets and made a tugging motion, as if he were trying to lift himself off his seat. He said seriously, and his words seemed to slur more than before. "Ah'm sorry, Mr. O'Brien, suh, but I jest don't seem to be able to move, suh."

"What are you playing at, man? What do you mean, you can't move?"

"Well, suh, Mr. O'Brien, suh, I figure it's going to need about an extra dollar a day to get my black arse up on that there seat. Suh." He was grinning now.

O'Brien was obviously restraining himself with tremendous difficulty. "Goddamn it, that's robbery," he ground out through his clenched teeth.

"Yes, suh," agreed his tormentor cheerfully. "Of course, you could always get a factory-trained engineer to help you out, couldn't you?"

"O'Brien knew when he was beaten," said Father. "Besides, taking him all around, he was a fair man, and he might have been a bit sorry for the way he had treated Black Jack, because he gave in with less fuss than I thought he would.

"'All right,' he says. 'I guess I deserved that. But I never thought I'd get my pocket picked this far from Cordova Street. Now get going and do your stuff.'"

Black Jack got up with no difficulty this time, a broad grin the only sign of his victory. He vaulted up on the sled, went directly to the boiler and threw a couple of dry logs in the firebox, then began to tie down the safety valve, looking at them comically out of the corner of his eye, and using somewhat exaggerated motions while doing it. The engineer growled something inaudible, clearly not a sound of approval.

Father reassured him. "Black Jack says there's nothing to worry about. He says the rivets will tell him if it's going to blow."

The man looked at Father incredulously. He said bitterly, "I'm going to pretend that I didn't hear that. If I heard it, I'd have to think about it, and I'm not going to think about it." He swung away with the air of one who has finished with a distasteful subject and doesn't intend to refer to it again.

The fire in the boiler was hot now and steam was up. Black Jack opened the steam valve and the engine responded instantly. He went through his moves while they watched, the engineer disdainfully, O'Brien expectantly, and Father, confidently. Then once again the taut line; nothing moving, no sound, just a sense of strain, and Black Jack listening, watching. Seconds went by, then a minute. The engineer made a dismissive motion, started to say something, but stopped as Father put out his hand.

"Look," he pointed. The line was beginning its strange, almost imperceptible motion like the scales of a snake's skin moving as its muscles tense. And then the drum began to turn, and the line was coming in, the tension eased, and all was normal, with the engine chuffing happily away.

The engineer cursed blasphemously.

O'Brien turned to him and said in challenge, "There. What do you say to that?"

"What I'd like to know," answered the other, somewhat plaintively, "is how does he know what's going on? How long to wait. The log could be stuck, and he'd sit there waiting all day!"

"He told me you have to feel it in your bones," Father put in helpfully.

The engineer shook his head in bafflement. "I came up here to show you how to work an engine, not to do black magic."

The BIRLING match

Logging sports seem not to have caught on in the world at large. The Olympics—summer or winter—don't include chopping, axe-throwing or tree-climbing among their events. More's the pity. There are times when the injection of a little mayhem might be beneficial. Admittedly, the skills required are somewhat specialized, and in a world increasingly short of trees, logging is not exactly an approved activity any more.

There are few mentions of logging sports that I'm aware of in accounts of the previous century, aside from isolated competitions amongst loggers, such as the log drives in some Quebec rivers. On the West Coast it seems not to have become a spectator sport until the early days of this century. Even here it was a rather specialized event, requiring some experience to appreciate the fine points involved in the various skills. The one exception was the sport of log birling. Anyone, young or old, no matter how inexperienced, can enjoy the attempt of two men to each roll the other into the water from a floating log. In BC, where almost every bay had a logging camp of some sort, with a boom crew to work on the logs once they were in the water, birling was the most popular logging sport. Each year, matches were held at all the major camps: Victoria, Campbell River, Courtenay and various others. Champions were proclaimed, belts and/or prizes awarded. Myrtle Point, near Powell River, was one of these centres, to which men came from all around for the annual summer competition. There was a strong feeling of rivalry between the camps of the mainland—Stillwater, Myrtle Point, etc.—and those opposite them on Vancouver Island. Among these, Fanny Bay, Union Bay and Comox were of particular note.

It was Father's favourite sport, and his crew at Myrtle Point were enthusiasts to the last man. Every evening, spring to summer, they would practise after supper in the pond by the log dump. Their practice log—eighteen feet long by eighteen inches thick—was kept on a rack behind the boom shack when not actually being used. Knotless, and light as foam, it floated like a duck's feather on the water. A spare one was kept ready behind the stove in the bunkhouse for when the other—roughened and torn by the sharp caulks—must be discarded. When needed, six men would carry it to the water by rope slings, and another log would take its place behind the stove.

Father won the champion's belt the first year he competed. His perfect coordination and wiry quickness made him a natural. He won again the following year. When I asked him to tell me about it, he shrugged, uninterested.

"It wasn't hard. Not many men can stay in balance all the time. You just wait, and at the right time, off they go!"

He left the camp at Myrtle Point then, but returned to defend his belt a third time. A man from his old boom crew spotted him.

"Hal, glad to see you. I knew you'd show up. I've been watching for you. What do you think of this fellow from Quebec everybody's talking about?"

It seemed to Father that everyone he'd met for the past month had asked him the same question, and he answered it as he had before. "I haven't seen him roll. I hear he's pretty good, though. Guess I'll soon know."

"Pretty good! I'll say he's pretty good! I saw him in a match down at Parksville a few weeks back. He made everyone look like fools! He says that if they had one of our logs back on the river where he comes from they'd throw a blanket on it and use it as a bed to sleep on. I think you're going to have your work cut out for you with that one!"

Father arrived early on the day of the competition, curious to see the man of whom he had heard so much. Some of the competitors were out on the "practice" logs, and already there was a crowd of people there, meeting acquaintances and watching. He was standing apart, trying to determine if any of the men on the logs looked good enough to be the one, when he heard someone behind him say, "Hal Hammond?"

He turned. "That's me."

He saw a man of medium size, but strongly built, every move giving the impression of restrained power. He took the sinewy brown hand offered him.

"Paul St. Jean, from the rivers of Quebec, at your service," said the man, smiling. "I hear you are the one I will have to beat, to win today."

(I have inferred the "St. Jean." Father pronounced it "Sanjan.")

The speaker had blonde hair, and a small moustache of the same light colour. He was very handsome.

Father was surprised. He had somehow formed the impression that everyone from Quebec had dark hair and swarthy skin.

The hand tightened, but relaxed quickly when there was no response. The smile widened. "Saving your strength, eh? That is well. Today, you will need all that you have. And that, my friend, will not be enough!" Laughing, the blonde man turned, not waiting for an answer, and stepped lightly away.

Father didn't know whether to be angry or amused, but finally settled for the latter. It was all done with such irrepressible good nature that anger didn't seem called for. Besides, he thought that his rival might have a surprise coming in a short while.

The time passed quickly, in spite of the usual confusions and delays that are an inevitable part of such occasions. At length the program came to log rolling. Father put on his boots, studded with gleaming new caulks, the soles oiled and flexible, the uppers soft as glove-leather. Each competitor had registered, and was assigned a number. Now the first numbers were being drawn. Care was taken to ensure that the last match would be between the two best men entered.

Father disposed of his first opponents with his usual efficiency, with much joking and some playing to the crowd just for the fun of it. The man from Quebec was paired off first with one of Father's old crew, a log roller of considerable skill, who lasted about ten seconds. The rest of the blonde Québécois' unfortunate draws did no better. He moved with a speed and ferocity that awed the crowd, and gave Father much to think about.

He told me, "I knew in my very bones, that no man born could roll me off a log. But, as I watched him move, I had a bad feeling that there was no way I could put that wildcat in the water."

At last, the final matchup was announced.

"And now, ladies and gentlemen, the one you've all been waiting for. From the rivers of Quebec, where if you fall in, you're dead; the man who claims he can ride anything that floats: Paul St. Jean. Matched with him in the final roll, our own Hal Hammond, champion of the coast, never defeated!"

(There was no "champion of the coast" at that time, I think. Only of each regional event. But announcers seldom worry about such matters.)

The crowd cheered. Bettors yelled encouragement to whichever man they had gambled on.

Father selected a pike pole from the ones provided,

fourteen feet of tough hickory wood. He stepped onto the log, walked to one end, and stood waiting. St. Jean leaped lightly onto the other end, placed the end of his pole against the float and shoved the log out into the pond with a heave of his powerful shoulders. They stood for a moment, eyeing each other curiously, alert for sudden moves, the log held motionless with practised ease.

"I've been watching you, boy," said the blonde man. "You're pretty good. Best I've seen out here. Show off a bit, but that's all right. So do I, so do we all, if we can."

Father smiled, but made no reply. He expected a trick, an attempt to take him off guard.

St. Jean held his pole out, hefting it lightly. "We have no need of these, eh? They only slow us down." With a quick move, he hurled it across the water and stood waiting. Most birlers relied on their poles for balance.

"Okay by me." Father did the same.

"Ha, good," approved the other. "Now we will see." As he spoke, he moved like a striking wolf, and the log leaped like a live thing.

"In the first few seconds," said Father, "I knew I'd met a master. He was at home on that log, and I was just a visitor there. I could stay on, but I couldn't even try to put him off. He spun the log so fast the water hissed like a rainstorm. Then he jumped in the air, spun around and came down facing the other way. When he landed, the log stopped dead in the water. It's a good trick, works every time if the other fellow isn't ready for it. But I knew he'd try it. What you have to do is jump and turn just after he does. When you come down, the log has stopped, and you're in position when it starts again."

Again the French-Canadian tried it—and variations of it—spinning back, and back again, in an erratic pattern that had the crowd yelling its approval. Suddenly, while still spinning the log, he ran swiftly to the other end just inches from Father, their combined weight sinking the log until they were in the water up to their knees.

"That was fine with me," said Father. "You can't move the log as quickly under water, and if he touched me he'd be disqualified. He must have thought he might force me into making a mistake, but he soon gave that up."

Twenty minutes passed, and then the blonde man stopped as abruptly as he had started. He stood there silently, rocking the log back and forth gently. He had done this before, then burst into a fury of motion that almost caught Father off guard, so he was ready for a similar trick this time. But instead, St. Jean turned to face the shore and raised both hands, palms out in an expressive shrug. Someone shouted, "It's a tie!" and the crowd roared. He crooked a finger, and someone threw him a pole, which he used to paddle the log over to the float. The judge—or referee—was there waiting.

"It's a tie, then?" he asked, voice hoarse from shouting. Father had jumped off the log when his opponent did, and was standing beside him. St. Jean threw an arm around him (causing him considerable embarrassment) and said, laughing, "No more, it would be boring. He is half limpet, this one, the way he stick to that log!"

The announcer held up his hand and shouted, "The match is a tie. The champion keeps his belt!"

Everyone applauded and hurrahed, for they were very parochial and would have hated a "foreigner" to have gone off with the prize.

The belt was handed to Father. The belt that he had won the previous year, and returned when he had registered for this match. (I saw the mate to it—just the buckle—when I was young, for he had been able to keep the first one he had won. It was a "picture" buckle showing two men on a log, their pike poles crossed as if they were quarterstaffs. Father wasn't much interested in it, and it was lost or given away before I thought to ask for it.)

He took the belt and stood there looking at it. It meant a lot to him then, and he had been proud to win it. He turned to the man from Quebec, and handed it to him.

"I don't deserve it," he said, voice pitched to carry. "I didn't earn it. All I did was stay on. You did all the work. By right, it should be yours."

There were sounds of dismay from the crowd. St. Jean took the belt by the buckle, ran his other hand quickly along the leather, so that the end made a snapping sound. He grinned widely, white teeth flashing under blonde moustache.

"It is right, what you say, and the right thing you do, and these people should know it. You are very good, better than I think, even. But it is true. All you can do is stay on the log." He laughed. "But that is a lot when Paul St. Jean is on the other end!" Then, placing one hand on Father's shoulder, he said seriously, "You should come to

Quebec with me, to the rivers of Quebec. In a year, or maybe two, you could be the greatest. Almost as great as Paul St. Jean, maybe." And laughing once again, he made his way among the people crowded around. Father never saw or heard of him again.

And never again did Father enter a log-rolling contest. "You see," he told me, "always before, I thought I was the best. I thought that if there was a prize for log rolling, it was only right that I should have it. But then I met him, and I knew that I'd never get to be that good. So wherever I went, if I won a prize, I'd know that I only won it because he wasn't there; that it really belonged to him. And I didn't want to do that—to feel like that. So I quit."

I considered it a rather strange attitude to take. But Father thought strangely at times.

EPILOGUE

It is many years later. We are living in the small town of Gibson's Landing. Father is now seventy years old and still active. We work together at log salvage, or "beachcombing."

The Chamber of Commerce, or whatever the equivalent, has decided to organize a "Sea Festival." Among the events will be log birling. There are many log-sorting operations in the sheltered waters of Howe Sound, employing a total of perhaps sixty or eighty boom men. Machinery hasn't yet superseded skill on logs, and the quality of competition is expected to be high. The organizer of this part of the festival was Fred Holland, both friend and hunting companion to Father. Knowing that Father had once birled, and that we had always a store of logs, he asked if we would pick out something suitable to use in the event.

Father took the task very seriously. His professional expertise was being enlisted and he meant to spare no trouble. We had nothing on hand that he felt was right for the occasion, so we made the rounds of all the beaches, looking for the perfect log. They were plentiful on the shores in those days and we found a dry, high-floating cedar without much trouble. We pulled it out of the water onto our other logs, where Father chose a knot-free section, measured it carefully, and we cut it to length. When it was back in the water he looked at it critically, then, taking his pike pole and jumping on it he spun it underfoot, first one way and then the other, finally pushing it into a corner where he secured it.

"It's a bit slow," he judged, "but I guess it'll do. If it's too quick, the matches may not last long enough to get the people interested."

Then he picked out a larger, longer log, a fir with bark on it that floated quite a bit lower in the water.

"We'll give them this one too," he decided. "The kids can have some fun pretending to be log rollers."

On the morning of the big day, we towed the logs to the picnic area. No one was there, so we tied them up and left. We had work to do that day, so we didn't attend the event, but the next day we went back to get the logs. Fred was there, cleaning up. They stood for a moment, talking of the previous day.

"How did the birling go?" Father asked him.

"Oh, it was a lot of fun. A real crowd-pleaser. Some of those fellows were really good. They said the log was a bit quick, though. Some of them didn't last long on it." He pointed. "It was a good notion of yours to bring the little cedar there over for the kids. They had a great time trying to get up on it. A couple of the men tried to use it, but they soon gave that up!"

Living Off the Land

"You've got to come, Hal," Shorty Roberts said excitedly. "It'll be a great hunt. Country even you've never hunted. And just think, man, a chance to get a bighorn!"

"Who told you there were bighorns there?" asked Father skeptically.

"Judd Johnstone said they've seen them lots of times. They winter there, some herd that's wandered down from the interior. No one else knows about them. You go up the Skwaka about twenty miles, then cut back up the hill on the left side. You angle back a few miles up the side valley and there's a lake there about a mile long. He says the sheep winter there around the lake."

"Did Judd say they'd ever shot one of these bighorns? He never mentioned it to me if he did."

"Well, no, I don't think he actually shot one. Maybe the season wasn't in or something."

"I never knew that to stop Judd, or his brothers either," commented Father. "That's wild country up there. Bad enough in good weather, and we aren't going to have much more of that. We're due for snow in those valleys anytime now. I think I'll just stay down here where it's warm. Thanks, anyhow."

"But you've got to come, Hal. I wouldn't feel safe in the woods with that bunch, and I really want to see what's in there. I'll probably never get another chance at a bighorn. We need someone who knows his way around that kind of country."

"Who all is going?"

"Well, besides Frank and Stan, there's that young fellow who works at the store, Harold his name is, and the Edwards brothers. Oh yeah, and that young schoolteacher that quit and went logging. I think his name is Phil something or other."

"That," said Father, "isn't a hunt, it's an expedition. Why didn't you invite the rest of Pender Harbour along? You could surround the sheep like they do with animals in Africa!"

"It's not that bad. Just the eight of us, if you come along," his friend said somewhat defensively. "Your boat can hold eight easily."

"Aha," said Father, "it's not just me. I thought there was a catch. You need a boat, and the only other one is that floating wreck of Frank's."

"Now, you know better than that, Hal; we really want you to come. If you don't, you know those fellows are going to get in trouble back there, maybe even some of them killed, and it'll be your fault."

Father was always too soft-hearted for his own good. He agreed to think about it. That was enough for Shorty. He considered the matter settled.

"That's great," he enthused. "I knew you couldn't resist it. I'll tell Frank tomorrow and you can talk it over with him. It's his idea, really."

So they left it at that, and in the next day or so, Father met with Frank and they settled on the date. Frank was a large rangy man in his thirties, who ran a small A-frame logging show with his partner Stan. He was used to bossing a crew of men, and had a loud voice and a confident manner. He talked enthusiastically of hunting, and minimized the difficulties of the trip.

"Why," he said confidently, "it's just a little hike in the woods. There's always deer and bear trails up and down those river valleys. Never fails. Just have to pick the ones that are going the right way!"

"Well," said Father, "that's not always as easy as it might be, but we'll sure give it a try."

"I thought," he told me, "that here was a man who had a lot to learn, and it might be fun to see him learning it."

The day arrived and with it, the would-be sheep hunters. Just six of them, as one of the Edwards brothers couldn't make it.

Father took the bed-rolls as they were handed to him. He hefted one. It was much too light.

"Where's your food, and who's got the cookware?" Frank heard him say.

"Oh, didn't I tell you? We're going light. No food. We'll live off the land, shoot what we need on the way. That's the way the Johnstone brothers do it, and if they can, well I guess we can."

Father looked them over critically. "Well, you don't look much like the Johnstone boys, and you haven't spent your lives learning to live like they do when they hunt. It should be an interesting trip."

As he said to me, "I figured it would also be a short trip. About two days without food would see a big difference in their attitude."

So off they went, sixty miles to the head of Jervis Inlet and the valley of the Skwaka River.

Arriving finally at the river mouth, Father eased the boat's bow into the shore near the left bank and got rid of his load of hunters. Then he double-anchored the boat and rowed ashore in the skiff to join them. As he was leaving the boat, he slipped a couple of chocolate bars into his coat pocket.

When he rejoined the party, they were arguing over which side of the river to go up.

Father said later, "I had decided to have as little as possible to do with making decisions. It was their trip, I was just going along for the ride."

However, when Shorty asked, "What do you think, Hal? You know the country," he pointed out that if he had thought the right-hand side of the valley the better way, he would have landed them on that bank, but there were swamps on that side, and they would have had to cross over the big tributary stream called the Hunechin, about half a mile up on the right.

So that was decided, and off they went, Frank in the lead, watching for one of the trails he was so confident of finding. And soon he did find one, a typical river-valley bear trail, redolent of the decaying carcasses of spawning salmon deposited there by the bears who had made it. But the trouble with a bear trail, as they soon learned, is that a bear walks on all fours, and the brush above about three feet is mostly unbroken. Also, rather than going straight up the valley, the bear tends to wander into the nearest swamps where it spends much of its time.

After a couple of hours of this, the sweating, cursing, hunting party had had enough. Frank's partner was the first to give in. A heavyset man, muscular but with a layer of fat from good eating, he was red-faced and dripping as if a bucket of water had been emptied over his head. He threw himself down on a moss-covered log and said loudly, his voice near desperation, "By Christ, there has to be a better way than this! Where are those trails you were talking about?"

The others had flung themselves down wherever they were when they stopped, except Father, who could slip through brush like an eel through seaweed, and Shorty, who could walk all day without any obvious show of effort.

Frank was also on his feet, flushed of face and sweating almost as much as his partner.

"I can't understand it. These valleys are supposed to be full of trails. There can't be much more of this. We should hit easier going anytime now."

"It gets worse," said Father cheerfully. "We've been

in the easy stuff. Wait'll you see what it's like in another mile. The devil's club is so thick even the bears go around it!" (This was a slight exaggeration.) His companions groaned or cursed as their nature dictated. Shorty spoke up.

"Well, what do we do? We can't go on like this."

"You have to read the land," answered Father. "Some places it's clear if you stay right on the river's edge. In others the flats aren't bad going. Some places you have to go up on the sidehills to get by, which isn't bad either, unless you hit boulder patches."

"Well, I give up," rasped Frank in frustration, "If you know so much about it, show us how to do it."

"Okay," answered Father. "But there's no easy way, you know. You're not on a logging road now," he added, with just a touch of malice. "And remember to keep an eye out for supper. It'll be dark in a couple of hours and I haven't noticed much in the way of food so far."

The others said nothing, but looked around them with new interest. They had forgotten that they were going to live off the land.

"With seven of us crashing along in the brush," Father added, "even the squirrels will take cover." He walked up past where Frank was standing, and led the way to the river bank. The brush was thinner right on the edge, and they began to make somewhat better time.

At last, the shadowed places under the trees began to grow darker. It was only four o'clock, but there was a heavy cloud layer. Father knew that full dark was only about half an hour away. He threw his blanket roll under the shelter of a spruce tree that would shed all but the heaviest rain. The others looked at him.

"Why are we stopping?" inquired one of them. It was the young man whose name was Harold. He had kept up well enough, but he looked weary.

"You have about a half hour to find something for supper," announced Father.

"But . . . what is there to find?" It was Stan, obviously not used to foraging, but a hearty eater of what others provided.

"Maybe you can scare up a bear. If he doesn't get you before you get him. Bear steaks aren't bad. They'll taste of rotten fish now, though. They tell me you don't notice it after a couple of weeks. Or there might be a spawning salmon up one of these little side creeks."

"What are you going to eat?" challenged Frank.

"Me? Oh, I'm just going to tell my stomach that it isn't really hungry yet, and to quit bothering me." And with that, Father began to gather branches for a fire. A fire is a cheerful thing in the woods at night, even if there's nothing to cook on it. Young Harold stayed to help, and the others wandered somewhat aimlessly off in search of supper.

After the fire was going, Harold spoke, his voice a bit unsteady.

"You think we're just a bunch of crazy amateurs with no business being out here, don't you, Hal?"

"Well, not crazy," Father answered. "Not yet!"

There was shouting and splashing up the little stream just ahead of them. Shorty Roberts had elected to try there, accompanied by Stan and Reggie Edwards.

"Grab it, don't let it get away!" someone yelled.

More splashing. More shouting. Then silence. Presently they emerged from the brush. Stan was carrying a fish. He walked up to the fire and threw it down. There was a crashing of brush, as the other two entered the clearing, carrying nothing but their rifles.

Frank said, "Well, you got something. That's great. A salmon, eh?" He stopped by the fire, and they all stood there, looking down at the catch. It was a spawned-out dog salmon. There was not a spot of silver on it. Most of the scales were gone; its sides were gaunt and coloured muddy grey-black, where they weren't white with fungus. It was blind. Its fins and tail were eaten away with fungus, and ugly red patches of raw flesh showed on its back.

The men contemplated it silently. Stan said slowly, "I'm not that hungry."

Shorty Roberts said, "I wouldn't give that to my dog."

Frank looked around at the others. "Anyone want to try eating it?"

He picked up a stick, stuck it in the fish's gills, and carried it over to the river bank. There was a splash. He came back, slumped down by the fire and commented glumly, "Well, one thing about it, looking at that fish took away my appetite."

Father spoke up. "You'll wish you hadn't done that." No one answered him.

And that was the first day.

Father woke as the first tinge of grey lightened the night sky. He didn't have much liking for sleeping on the ground. As he once told me, "My bones are too close to my skin. I feel every twig and pebble under me. It takes a lot of time to make a really comfortable bed in the woods."

He nursed to life a few coals still smouldering in the remains of the fire, and soon had a nice cheerful blaze going. The others began to show a bit of life at the sight and sound of the fire, but the air was cold, and they weren't in any hurry to get out in it.

Father brought his travelling teapot out of an inner pocket. It was a cunningly made collapsible metal drinking cup which would serve to boil water. With it, he carried a little packet of tea leaves. He started off to fill it with water, then paused and called out, "Who has the coffee pot? Toss it here and I'll fill it."

Frank spoke up, sounding a bit less self-assured than usual.

"There isn't any coffee pot. We all agreed to rough it, to live off the land. We eat meat and we drink water, so we can prove that we haven't gone soft."

Father collapsed his 'teacup' and slipped it back into his pocket. He thought it might be well to save the tea for another time.

"Well," he commented, "at least there's lots of water."

It was a silent group of hunters who rolled up their blankets and left the warmth and cheer of the fire to head on up the river through the dew-soaked brush. An hour of walking brought them to a fair-sized branch creek.

Father said, "The going gets pretty rough for a while. I think we'd do better getting off the flat and working our way along the sidehill."

The schoolteacher, Phil, asked quietly, "How far

have we come, Hal? About twenty miles, would you say?" He hadn't spoken much except to young Harold, with whom he seemed to feel more at ease than with the older men. Father had wondered how he had come to be included, but never did find out.

"No, I'd say more like six miles."

They had all been listening for the answer to Phil's question and there was a shocked silence as Father started off at a brisk pace, following the course of the side creek. They crossed it on a fallen tree, and in a few more minutes were on the lower slopes of the side of the valley.

They were so happy to be out of the brush of the valley bottom that at first they didn't notice that the ground was mostly boulders, covered with moss so thick that it bridged many of the holes between them. Father warned them several times, but it took bruised shins to convince them not to step on the nice level spots. To muscles unused to this sort of up-and-down travel, the level ground they had left—however brush-covered—began to seem not so bad after all.

Suddenly, Father came to an abrupt stop, holding his hand up in the signal to stop moving. It took quite a few seconds for them all to see it and comply, as well as much threshing and peering as they all tried to see what was the matter.

He said quietly, "Listen." He had already swung his rifle to the ready position and now he pointed with it to a spot on the valley bottom just ahead and below them, and they heard the thump that is the warning signal of an alarmed deer. There it went, bounding off through the salmon brush, with just a glimpse of fast-moving grey showing now and then.

Father said later, "There were guns pointing in all directions. Nobody was ready to shoot. I never saw such an exhibition in all my life."

He had slipped his own gun back in carrying position, realizing that there was no chance of getting an effective shot, and he never shot unless he was sure of a kill.

Stan got off the first shot, but it was at the sky straight above him. He had gotten his rifle strap tangled in his bedroll, and somehow managed both to get the safety off and pull the trigger. That scared him so badly he gave up trying.

"Frank was pretty quick, I'll give him that," Father told me. He fired all eight shots in his magazine as fast as he could get them in the chamber. He didn't even try to aim, just fired into the brush in the hope of getting lucky."

He didn't.

Shorty got his rifle levelled with his usual efficiency, and saw the futility of it just as quickly. Reggie Edwards levered a cartridge into the chamber of his gun and immediately levered it out again, unfired. He picked up the unfired shell and gazed at it with immense astonishment. Phil, the teacher, got his gun off his shoulder fairly quickly and pushed frantically at the safety. After a few moments, he gave up in disgust.

"I don't know if he knew it or not" said Father, "but he was pushing it the wrong way. On, instead of off. Of course it was on already and wouldn't move."

Harold stood holding his gun in front of him, his

gaze abstracted. He told Father afterwards, "My mind just went blank. For the life of me I couldn't think what I was supposed to do next."

Frank reloaded frantically, then plunged down the hill.

"Come on!" he shouted, "spread out, we've got him trapped against the river bank."

They followed him, slipping and sliding down the hill, crashing wildly through the salmon brush at the bottom. Father and Shorty followed more deliberately. "It isn't safe down there," Father commented. "They'll blast anything that moves."

At last the frustrated hunters regrouped, having seen nothing. Father and Shorty joined them. Frank was saying, "I don't see how he got away from us. We had all the ground covered."

Father said, "That's easy. The first thing any deer would do is swim across the river to the other side. Check along the bank here and I'll bet you'll see where he jumped down." Which they did, and which they found.

Stan swore bitterly. "Damn it all to hell, I'm starving. I could eat half a deer all by myself!"

"Come on," urged his partner, "maybe we'll see another one. Keep your guns ready."

Reggie Edwards spoke up.

"I don't know about you fellows, but I'd rather plow through brush than go back on that hillside."

The vote was unanimous in favour of the brush. Father pointed out that their chances of seeing a deer were much less when they were surrounded by brush, and the noise they made would alert every animal in the valley, but even hunger wouldn't get them back on those mossy boulders.

It was now about noon. The sky had been getting darker all day as the clouds piled up between the mountains. A few flakes of snow began to slowly drift down. Frank chose to regard this as a good thing.

"Just what we needed," he enthused, his manner somewhat overdone. "We can spot fresh tracks easily in a couple of inches of snow, and they'll be a cinch to follow. And the sheep—we really need snow to make the sheep take to the trees where we can get at them. I was a bit worried that we'd have to climb to get to them, but this should do the trick."

Father made no comment. He didn't like the look of the weather at all. He considered they had gone far enough, but it was obvious that no one wanted to be the first to suggest that perhaps they should turn back.

Each time they stopped for a rest the only topic was food. Where to find it, how much there might be, and more and more about how much they would eat, given the opportunity.

At one stop, Harold asked, "You know about these things, Hal. What would the Indians do if they were here?"

"They wouldn't be here at this time of year; they're not stupid. But if they *did* get stuck out here, they'd make camp by the river, spear fish and smoke them. That dog salmon you threw away was just right. It would smoke really nicely."

The young man shuddered. "I wish I hadn't asked. Couldn't we do the same thing? Surely with this many of us we could catch a few fish to eat."

"We'd have to first find a pool with fish in it. For that we'd have to go back downriver a couple of miles to where the water runs slower. We'd have to rig up spears, which we don't know how to make properly. We'd have to find a spot where we could reach the fish. Most of what are left are coho and steelhead, and they are fast and spook easily. I don't think we could do it, do you?"

Frank said loudly, "Okay, then that's settled. We go on. We're bound to see tracks soon, and a couple of days without dinner aren't going to hurt us. Lead on, Hal."

Father looked around at the others. None of them said anything. The trouble was that Frank was one of those men who is used to giving orders, and who accepts obedience as his due. It takes a strong will to question such a man, and none of the others were prepared to do so just yet. Father could easily have done it, for he was a leader himself, but he didn't see why he should take the blame for aborting the hunt. After all, he was feeling no discomfort.

Shorty might have, but he was content to follow along with Father, who shrugged and started off once more.

The going was getting more difficult now, as the valley began to climb more steeply. There were no more flatlands, the valley walls in most places reaching to the edge of the river. The side they were on was becoming steadily more difficult, with broken rock and sheer precipices, so that when they came to where a big spruce had fallen across the river they crossed over it to the other side.

The major obstacles now were the slide areas, mostly caused by snow avalanching from the high slopes. The newer ones weren't bad, but the many old ones were favourite growth areas for mountain alder, a tough and tenacious tree that sends up multiple stems from ground level and may grow so thickly that you can almost walk on the tangled outspread branches. The rock underfoot, not having had time to settle, was loose and treacherous, while trees carried down by the slides made log jams by the river edge—where there was an edge, for the water was often split into three or four streams by piles of slide rock. The noise of water rushing through all that broken rock was almost deafening. If they had possessed enough energy to talk, they would have been obliged to shout.

They were crossing yet another slide, one with a fair-sized creek tumbling through the boulders. Where it hit the river's edge, there was enough of a flat spot for a large pool to have formed in the sand and gravel the creek had brought down. They were about a hundred yards uphill of the pool and had struggled about halfway across the strip of mountain alder bordering the slide area, when young Harold, who was walking behind Shorty, grabbed him by the arm and pointed to the pool. There, in a part of it that had been concealed from them until now, swam a big, beautiful Canada goose!

Father looked around on hearing Shorty's whispered "Hal." He held up his hand to stop the others, a finger at his lips for silence. He pointed. They all stared, entranced.

He made a motion of aiming a gun, then pointed to Frank, who had the newest rifle, equipped with a telescope sight. This was something rather unusual in those days and much envied by the others, except for Father himself who wasn't impressed by it; he considered it prone to fogging and being jarred out of alignment.

Frank raised his rifle to his shoulder and aimed for what seemed a long time.

They could see the gun barrel waving back and forth. They knew he was tired and cold, his fingers stiff, his footing uncertain. A downhill shot is a difficult one. What if he missed? He obviously couldn't face the thought. He lowered his gun and motioned violently to Father. Everyone had either seen Father shoot, or heard stories about his skill, and they were all looking at him now. He caught each one's eyes in turn, looking a question. They all declined promptly and unmistakably. He looked down. While this interplay had been going on, the goose had been feeding at the pool edge, quite unconcerned. In the roar of the water it had probably not even noticed the considerable noise they had made. Perhaps it didn't care.

Father eased the hammer back on his 38:55, sighted, fired. The goose head seemed to explode. He had disdained to play it safe and spoil the meat by a shot in the body.

Everyone shouted with joy and relief.

"Great shot," said Shorty.

"Goose for supper," from Stan.

Frank said nothing but plunged down the hill to retrieve the bird. It was flopping in the water in that death flurry that takes birds when they have been shot in the head and killed instantly. Frank should have gone back the fifty feet to the rock slide, and then down the rocks to the river. He chose instead to go directly down through the tangled mountain alder, which now was covered with about three inches of snow. It was not a good plan. He was a heavy man, strong and determined, but not especially agile. He kept slipping off the springy stems and having to climb up again from the ground, some seven or eight feet below. About halfway down he stopped for a moment.

His partner shouted "Hurry up, man, you'll lose it!"

They had noticed that the dead bird's struggles had carried it the few feet out to where the current from the little creek was swiftest. Frank yelled something and plunged on, only to disappear in a flurry of arms, legs and branches. He went in more or less head first, and it took him precious moments to surface. He flung himself on again, covering the rest of the distance on his chest and belly, using a sort of breast stroke over the yielding snow-covered branches, and landing finally in an untidy heap on the sand bank beside the water. Leaping to his feet, he raced to where the pool spilled into the river, just in time to see the goose caught up by the foaming current of the main rapids, where it bobbed along through the boulders faster than a man could run on level ground. There was nothing in sight to stop it, and in seconds it wasn't to be seen at all.

Frank stood there looking at the river, then he raised his arms over his head, his fists clenched, and giving a great yell of pure rage he cursed the goose, the river, the valley, the weather, and the bad luck that he thought was dogging him personally as the leader of the hunt. When his imagination failed him he stood for a moment looking down the river, then walked over to the slide, trudged up the hill and across to where the men stood waiting.

"All right," he said. "Let's get moving."

By now Father had had quite enough of this nonsense. They weren't even halfway to the lake where the sheep were supposed to be, and he knew the country ahead to be steep, rocky, and full of canyons. Difficult enough at any time, it would be quite impossible for tired and hungry men to cover in the snow. Shorty edged up to him and said, keeping his voice low, "Do you think they'll listen to reason yet, Hal?"

Father answered just as quietly.

"Frank is too mad to listen to anything just at the moment. There isn't enough light left to go back to a good spot anyhow. But don't worry," he added. "we've come about as far as we're going to."

He led them at an angle uphill to where a patch of good-sized hemlock and yellow cedar trees were growing on a bit of flat ground below a steep rock face.

They plodded after him, their clothes white with snow, not even bothering to look around, no doubt every one of them wishing earnestly that he was somewhere else.

Once in the shelter of the trees, he watched for a place to camp, and was pleased to see several likely spots. They approached a house-sized boulder, with a good overhang on the split-off side. Two extra large

mountain hemlocks grew beside it, their dense branches offering additional shelter. There were plenty of
dead branches for wood, as well as several small fallen
dry snags. Father stopped, threw off his bedroll and
announced, "All right, end of trail. We won't find a better place to camp tonight."

They accepted his word without question. Even Frank
flung down his blankets without hesitation. Father took
his belt axe out of its leather case and soon had a fire
started near the rock face. They all carried wood, until
there was a good-sized pile. Then they stood or sat
around the fire, their wet clothes steaming. They were a
quiet bunch of men compared to the first day.

Stan moaned, "God, I wish we had that goose roast-
ing over the fire!"

"That little bird wouldn't be enough to half fill you
up, let alone the rest of us," joked Reggie.

That set them off on the subject of food.

"It had only been two days," Father remarked to me,
"but you would think they had been starving for a
week. Hunger hits people in different ways. I was pretty hungry the first day, but I made up my mind that
there wasn't going to be any food for awhile and I can't
say I really missed it all that much. I wouldn't even
chew huckleberry buds because it would make my
stomach realize it was empty! Shorty, of course, never
complained about anything, except maybe if there
wasn't enough hunting to suit him. But the others, all
they could think of after the first day was food. They
thought about it so much that they talked themselves
into thinking they were starving to death. It's a mistake

to go on about something when you know you can't do anything about it."

After a while they all grew silent, tired even of the subject of food, and finally crawled with wet clothes into wet blankets. Only Father, Shorty, and somewhat surprisingly, Harold had brought oiled waterproof covers for their bedrolls, which now also served as groundsheets. The others had apparently assumed it never rained in Jervis Inlet. Fortunately for them, wool retains its heat even when wet, so they weren't totally miserable.

With the valley full of snowclouds, darkness came earlier than usual. The fire crackled and flickered and cast strange shadows. A few hundred feet below them, the river roared unceasingly, hypnotically. Snowflakes drifted through the branches, and in the spaces between the trees, snow lay six to eight inches deep. The sparks whirled up into the night, moving strangely in the gusts of wind. Father lay watching and listening, apparently the only one who appreciated the wild beauty of it all. At last, he too drifted off to sleep, lulled by the soft hissing of the snow.

He woke—as usual—at daylight. A few snowflakes were still falling. Though the trees had sheltered them from the worst of it, there was an inch or two of snow on everything, and it was fully two feet deep in the open spaces. He rose and rolled up his blankets in the oilskin groundsheet. Then he got his gun from the dry place where he had leaned it.

Harold had been watching. He said quietly, "Shall I get the fire going, Hal?"

"Might better let them sleep, unless you're too cold. There's the axe when you need it." He pointed to where he'd stuck it into a tree. "I'm going to mosey around and see if I can scare up some meat for breakfast." And off he went, following the little bench they were camped on, keeping under trees where he could, or near the overhanging rock face where a deer might be taking shelter from the snow. He moved slowly, ready to try a snap shot if he had to. The flat went farther than he had supposed, and it took almost two hours before he came to where it finally tapered out altogether. He began to work his way back by another route. He saw nothing. The snow was too deep, too fresh. Animals would stay where they were for awhile.

When he arrived back at the campsite, everyone was awake, standing around a fire that was two or three times as big as it needed to be.

Shorty said, "Glad you're back, Hal. I was beginning to think you'd fallen off a cliff or something."

Stan said, "Didn't hear any shots. Some deer hunter."

"No one can get them if they're not there," Shorty spoke up, ready in his friend's defence. Father placed his gun near the fire, and stood beside it. He wasn't cold, but his wool pants were soaked. As his clothes began to steam, he looked around the group.

"Where's Phil?" he asked.

No one answered for a moment. They looked about them as if he was hiding behind someone. Harold ventured, "He was here about half an hour ago. He stood by the fire, but he never said a word. I thought he looked kind of strange, but we all got to talking about what we'd like for breakfast and I sort of forgot about him."

Shorty added, "I saw him wander off in that direction. I figured he was going behind a rock, and I never thought anymore about it."

"What a bunch of muttonheads," Father accused them bitingly. And to Frank, "At least you should have kept an eye on him. You brought him out here. You know he's not as strong as the rest of us, and that he pushed himself too hard yesterday. If he falls and breaks a leg or something out here, we'll have a fine time packing him back to the boat."

Frank yelled, "Phil! Phi-i-l-l!"

They all listened. Nothing. Father picked up his gun. He said, "Wait here. I'll go find him."

Reggie Edwards spoke up, "We'll come too."

"No, you won't. I don't want any more of you floundering around out there and getting hurt or lost." When Father spoke in that manner, people tended not to argue. Reggie sat down again.

Father walked out in the direction Shorty had pointed. The tracks were plain in the fresh snow. They headed up valley, but angled downhill toward the river. He followed them at that ground-eating pace of his that was so deceptive.

"I knew he was out of his mind," Father said later. "I'd seen it happen before, and for less reason. I just hoped he wasn't so far gone that he might walk off the top of a cliff or something. But I saw when he came to a steep spot, that he took the logical way around it. He wasn't travelling fast, but he didn't stop either, and it took me a good twenty minutes to catch up with him.

He was floundering along in the brush and snow beside the river, heading up the valley. The going there wasn't so bad, but there was a nasty steep gully up ahead.

"I came up to him and called 'Hey, Phil!'

"He said, and his voice sounded as if he wasn't paying much attention, "Hello, Hal." He didn't stop. I asked him, 'Where do you think you're going?'

"'I'm going back to the boat.' He sounded as if he thought it was a silly question.

"'You're going in the wrong direction. The boat's back that way.'

"'Oh, no, it's just around the corner there. We'll see it any minute now.'

"He stumbled and fell pretty heavily, but he was up in a moment and off again, still heading up the valley. I walked around in front of him and took him by the shoulders and held him from going any farther, but his feet didn't stop moving. He kept on walking in the same place. He was looking straight at my face, but he didn't seem to see me. His eyes were focused away, beyond me. It made me feel queer. I said, 'Think man, how can you get to the boat from here, going uphill?'

"He didn't hear what I was saying. He just answered in that quiet voice, 'It's just over there a little ways.'

"I took one hand off his shoulder, and gave him a stinging slap on the cheek. His feet stopped moving. He looked at me in surprise, really looking this time. He said, 'What did you do that for?' Then he looked around him. 'What are we doing here? Where are the others?'

"'They're about half a mile back and uphill. You went on a little hike upriver by yourself, and I'm afraid you've got turned around a bit.'

"He looked back, and then he just collapsed in the snow. He groaned, 'I'll never make it. I never imagined I could be so tired and cold and hungry. I think I'd sell my soul for something to eat!'

"And I thought suddenly of the two chocolate bars in my pocket. I reached in, pulled one out, handed it to him and said, 'Oh, I don't think you'll have to do that.'

"He looked at it as though he didn't know what he was seeing. Then he ripped the paper off with his teeth and took a bite of it. I don't know when I ever saw a man's face change like his did then. Just that one bite made a new man of him. And I'll give him credit. He didn't hog the rest of it down. He ate it little bit by little bit, and then he looked at the paper and licked off a bit of chocolate that was stuck to it. He crumpled it in his fist and threw it over his shoulder.

"'Come on,' he said. 'We'd better get started back.'

"That chocolate bar acted like magic on him. And in a way, I guess it was. He wasn't really all that tired and hungry and weak. He just thought he was. But after all, he'd had a good night's sleep. It was only the third day without eating. Anyone can stand that! But he got to thinking too much about it, and how far he was from home, and it got to him. But the chocolate somehow made him forget all that, and he realized that he wasn't too tired to walk after all."

They started back, following their own trail, for it is always easier in snow to follow known ground rather than to break through fresh snow and risk new pitfalls.

And then, about halfway back, Father caught a glimpse of movement from the corner of his eye, almost missing it. He turned quickly, as a deer took half a dozen bouncing jumps through the snow from a little clump of trees in which it had been sheltering about a hundred feet uphill from them. Then it stopped and stood there for a moment, wondering which way to go next. Father flicked off his right-hand mitten and swung his rifle up in that fluid movement that always so impressed me whenever I saw it, thumbing the hammer back as his hand went through the trigger guard, firing as the sight was just reaching the target. The blast of the heavy rifle echoed from the mountain slopes, but the deer never heard the shot that killed it, for the bullet travelled faster than the sound.

The young schoolteacher looked around in bewilderment. The deer had fallen out of sight, and he couldn't imagine why Father had fired. Hesitantly, he asked, "Were you signalling them? I mean, the others?"

Father laughed, and headed up toward the deer. He wasn't in a hurry; he knew the shot was good.

He told me, "When we got up there, we saw a little spike buck, hit right where I'd aimed, just under the ear where there was no meat to be spoiled. I took out my knife to bleed it, and then I thought, no, blood is food too, and put the knife back again. The deer would only weigh about ninety pounds, and we'd need every ounce we could get."

He slung it over his shoulder, not bothering even to field dress it, and continued on up the hill.

In a few minutes they saw two figures emerge from the trees where the men were camped, and come floundering down the hill as fast as they could go. They were close enough to have seen that Father was carrying something.

The first one to arrive was Frank, having left Stan some distance behind him, puffing and blowing with the effort of keeping up with his partner's long legs.

Frank looked at the deer and said, "Nice going, Hal." Then to Phil, "You damned fool, what's the idea of doing a damned fool thing like that. You had us all worried we might have to pack you back to the boat."

Phil just looked sheepish and uncomfortable. He didn't answer. By then, Stan had arrived. He had eyes only for the deer, and he was almost crooning as he said, "Let me carry him. I want to feel the weight of all that meat on my shoulders."

Father was quite willing to give up his burden. Carrying almost a hundred pounds uphill on rough ground through two feet of snow was no pleasure.

"Stan wasn't a bad sort," judged Father, "but he was ruled by his stomach. He'd have fought a grizzly with his bare hands if it had tried to get that deer from him."

In a short while they were back at the fire. Stan hadn't stopped for a moment, even to catch his breath. He seemed, like the bears he rather resembled, to go better uphill than down.

"I'll never," Father said to me, "forget what happened then. I saw a bunch of men turn into a pack of wild animals, or a flock of vultures. You couldn't see the deer at all as they slashed away at it with their knives. I'll never know why there weren't fingers lost there that day. And then the rush to get sticks and hold the chunks over the fire. I couldn't believe my eyes. They didn't even take the hide off. I got a whiff of singed hair that almost turned my stomach. And then Stan dropped his piece in the fire. He yelped like a dog that's been kicked, and reached in with his hand to pull it out. Of course he burned his fingers and licked them, and he got a taste of the burned meat. That was enough for him. He tore off a big bite of raw meat and wolfed it down. Blood covered his cheeks and dripped off his chin! It was enough to sicken a wolf. And the rest were just as bad. As soon as they smelled burning meat, they couldn't wait. I decided then that I wasn't hungry."

Only Shorty had a thought for the man who had provided the meat and who was standing there watching them eat it. He looked around and said, "Come on, Hal, if you wait too long, there won't be much left."

Father replied ruefully, "I seem to have somehow lost my appetite," and he looked pointedly at Stan, who was just then trying to cram a piece of raw meat into a mouth too full to accept it.

Shorty grinned. He said, "You always did have a tender stomach. Oh well, maybe they'll leave you a bone to chew on."

At last, as Father put it, "They began to act a bit more like men instead of animals. They left the meat over the fire long enough that it didn't bleed when they bit into it. I know, dead meat doesn't bleed, but when it's only a few minutes since it was alive, and you bite at it, the blood drips out fast enough. They nibbled at that deer for another hour or so, but the pieces kept getting smaller and better cooked. I never realized that men could eat that much fresh meat. I fully expected them to sick it up, but not one of them did, although there were a few groans, mostly from Stan. You wouldn't believe me if I told you how much that man ate. I can hardly believe it myself!"

They even offered him a choice piece or two, nicely blackened, but he declined as politely as he could. He said, "I didn't like the smell of it. It smelled of burnt hair and hide."

They didn't insist very hard. There wasn't that much left after all.

They built up the fire again, and they all sat there soaking up the warmth, their stomachs heavy with the almost-raw meat.

Suddenly, after a particularly long silence, Frank spoke. "Well boys, I guess the great sheep hunt is over. For this year, anyhow. We might as well head for home. What do you say, Hal?"

"I say we should have headed home yesterday morning, or better still, we should have stayed home in the first place. These valleys are no place to be, this time of the year. Even the trappers make sure they have their cabins full of food for the winter by now. As for heading for home, I don't think we'll be doing much of that today. In fact, I think we'd better hole up right where we are for awhile."

They all looked at him in amazement.

"What are you talking about?" demanded Frank belligerently.

Father pointed at the sky. In the past half hour the clouds had begun to move. Now they were streaming up the valley, driven by a gale of southeast wind. He pointed through a gap in the trees. Snowflakes, like veils of white smoke were sweeping up the valley, and right on cue, big wet flakes of snow began to fall all around them.

He unrolled his blankets, spread them on the groundsheet, and slid beneath them.

"Might as well turn in," he said. "It's going to be a long day."

And a long day it was. They slept, and kept the fire going, and tried to sleep even when they no longer needed to. There was some attempt at the storytelling that is so much a part of a normal hunting trip, but there is a time and mood for that, and this wasn't the time and they weren't in the mood.

And it snowed and snowed.

At three in the afternoon it was already almost dark. Reg went out into the nearest open spot and came back slapping snow off himself. He looked worried, and he sounded even more worried.

"It's up to my hip pockets out there," he announced. "If this keeps up we'll be snowed in. We'll never get through it. It'll be up over our heads."

There was a chorus of alarmed exclamations, even a heartfelt "Geez" from Shorty. Frank turned to Father.

"What are we going to do, Hal?"

The answer came somewhat drowsily.

"I don't know about you, but I'm going back to sleep."

"No, but really, how are we going to get out if it keeps on snowing all night?"

Father had little patience with this sort of thing. He turned to face them, propped up on one elbow.

"Well, there's usually a good hard frost about Christmas. We could walk out on the crust then. But don't worry. A week or so without eating, you'll be so thin you'll be able to walk on fresh snow without leaving a mark!"

He told me, "No one seemed to think this was funny, so I turned back over and pretended to go to sleep. You should have heard them; they were going to make skis, they were going to make snowshoes, they were going to raft down the river, they were going to make sleds. I guess I should have spoken up and put them out of their misery, but it was as good as a picture show to hear them talk, and it gave me something to listen to until I finally did fall asleep."

Next morning, as he had known it would, the warm southeast wind pushing up the valley turned the snow to rain, and there was less snow on the ground than there had been the night before.

But it wasn't a happy camp. The rain and melting snow was now coming through the bushy trees that had sheltered them until then. Those who had no groundsheet were lying in blankets which were becoming more sodden the longer they lay in them. It took about an hour to get the fire going, and when it did, it smoked. They snarled at each other for almost any reason, and quarrelled viciously over the distribution of the rest of the deer. The best meat was gone; what was left was stringy and tough. Only Stan didn't complain about it. Nevertheless, they all finished their share, and looked around for more, even though they knew there wasn't any.

By eleven o'clock, the snow had shrunk to a depth of about two feet. It was heavy and stuck to shoes or anything else that touched it, but it was now passable.

"Well," said Father to the glum crew attempting to dry their bedding at the totally inadequate fire, "we'd better get going if we're going to make it back to a decent place to camp tonight."

They looked at him without enthusiasm.

"You mean you expect us to walk in that stuff?" asked Stan in dismay.

"You don't have to leave this nice dry camp just because I'm going," Father answered reasonably. "Of course you may have a bit of trouble getting enough wood without an axe, but I'm sure you'll manage somehow. I think you'll be warmer walking than staying here, though. In fact I expect you'll work up quite a sweat wading through this snow."

There was some grumbling, but they knew well enough that they couldn't stay where they were, and without too much delay they were off. After all, they didn't have much gear to pack up.

Father was right, as usual. In a half hour they were all sweating, and cursing the wet slippery snow. The weight of it did keep some of the brush pressed down, but it also concealed the holes, which were often as deep as their waists. The rain and melt filled all the draws with water, and they had to wade up to their hips where it had only been ankle deep on the way in. Not that this mattered much, they were soaked anyhow, but the water in their wool clothing was a lot warmer than melted snow.

The mountain alder on the slide had been bad on the way in, but covered with two feet of wet snow it was almost impossible to fight through. They floundered over it on their bellies, fell through, had to be pulled out and fell through again. In three hours, Father figured they'd made less than two miles, and the shadows were already getting darker. The rain still fell, and they were too tired to work hard enough to get warm. It was time to camp, but there was no place to take shelter from the freezing rain. Some of the men were starting to panic. Even Shorty sounded worried.

"We'll never make it back to camp," he said in a low voice meant for Father's ears only. They were a little ahead of the others.

"Oh, I don't think things are as bad as all that," Father reassured him. "Tell them to stick it out for a few more minutes."

He said, "I had kept a sharp eye out on the way in for places to make camp. It never hurts to know how far you have to go to shelter; it may save your life. I knew that there was a big cedar tree ahead that had fallen and shattered on the rocks and I'd figured on reaching it that day. We'd made less time than I'd thought we would, but we were just about there. I knew there would be dry cedar for a fire and there would be good shelter."

They just made it before dark. Wet, cold, tired and

hungry, it was a glum and silent group of men that threw down their soaked bedding and stood there waiting for someone to tell them what to do. But they were luckier than they knew, or deserved. Their camp was ready and waiting. The cedar tree, about eight feet through, had broken at the base. The first sixty feet or so had split in half and the halves had separated, but they were still joined on the underside by some bark and sapwood. This split trunk was held about head high from the ground by the boulders it had fallen on. The rest of the tree, almost to the top, had hit the ground harder and had shattered, creating all the firewood they could ever want.

Father directed some of them to gather wood, others to brush out the largest space under the split trunk and between the boulders, while he shaved off dry slivers and got a fire going—a long one, so that they could all get in front of it and spread out their blankets to dry.

In minutes, they were all standing by the fire, their clothes and blankets throwing off clouds of steam. They were almost cheerful, until Stan remembered that there was nothing to cook on the fire. He punched himself on the head, groaning.

"Do you realize, fools that we are, we left a perfectly good deer head back there? There's a good meal on that head; brains, eyes, ears, they're all food. And then there's the guts. They could be scraped and fried. The way I feel now, I could cut the hide in strips and eat it! Why in hell didn't we think to bring it with us?"

Frank scowled at him.

"You fool, you just barely managed to drag yourself

this far, as it is. How do you think you'd have managed carrying a deer's head and guts?"

His partner was unconvinced. "We could have taken turns."

But Frank had the last word.

"If you hadn't made such a pig of yourself, we could have had a load of good solid deer meat. Deer guts!" He snorted contemptuously.

This time there was no reply. One by one they rolled up in their wet but warm blankets, as near to the fire as they could get, and fell into the sleep of the exhausted.

Father and Shorty sat a while longer, throwing chunks of wood on the fire and talking.

"How much longer to the boat do you figure, Hal?"

Father pondered for awhile. Finally he said, "Oh, I don't know, Shorty. With a bit of luck we should be there by dark tomorrow."

But their luck turned out to be the wrong kind: bad.

In the night, the southeast storm died. The rain didn't stop, but as the cold valley air began to flow toward the sea, it turned once more to snow. By noon, that had stopped, but there was another foot of it over the old.

"By now," said Father, "even I was getting worried."

They woke to frost, cold enough to make them miserable, but not cold enough to crust the snow for walking. The fire was out, and no one wanted to get up and start another when there was nothing to cook on it anyhow. Harold was the one who finally made the effort.

"He was turning out all right," commented Father. "He had more gumption than the older men, who should have been the ones to set a good example."

For his part, Father didn't think he should play nursemaid to the rest of them, a view that was probably shared by Shorty.

"The more you do for a bunch like that, the more they'll let you do," was his way of putting it.

As the dry cedar pieces began to crackle and throw off some heat, the rest of them gathered around. They didn't say much. They didn't even have the heart to talk about food.

"By and large, though they were in pretty good shape, considering," said Father. "Even the schoolteacher had found his second wind, and seemed lively enough, for him."

Reg spoke up.

"Well, Hal," he said, "what are we going to do? Should we make a try for it?"

"There are two or three things we can do. I can go to the boat and bring some food back. I should be able to get back by dark. With something in our bellies we should be able to make it out the next day, if it doesn't snow again. Or, we can make a try for it right now, taking turns at breaking trail. Or, I can scout around and maybe find a deer. Take your pick."

"Why can't we all scout around and look for a deer?" asked Frank, with a hint of truculence. "Or at least those who feel like it."

Father was blunt. "That's bad ground down there, and I don't want a bunch of greenhorns floundering around and getting into trouble. It's a treacherous place if you don't know it, and you don't. Besides, Stan's hungry enough to see horns on a hat and I don't intend to be served up for supper."

There was a bit of grumbling, but as I have said before, few people argued with Father when he spoke in that tone. Shorty threw some wood on the fire and they all moved closer around it.

Father took his gun from the dry spot where he had leaned it, tried the action, and levering a shell into it ready for a fast shot, turned and headed diagonally up valley toward the river. Behind him, Stan called, "If it moves, shoot it."

But nothing moved. There were no tracks, not the least sign of any game. The snow was too fresh, too deep, and the deer—if there were any—still weren't moving. After an hour or so of pushing through the brush and snow he had had enough, and turned back toward camp. He was almost there when the sound of three evenly spaced shots from a heavy gun came from a bit farther down the valley. He hurried on as fast as he could, reaching the log just as three more shots sounded, sending echoes booming from the valley walls. Three spaced shots—the hunter's distress signal.

At the campsite, they were all standing out in the snow talking excitedly, looking down into the trees. All that is, except Stan and his partner. They were gone.

Father was amongst them before they knew he was there. Shorty was the first to notice him.

"I couldn't stop them, Hal," he said apologetically. "As soon as you left, Frank said, 'Who does he think he is, telling us what to do? I'm going to go look for some food.' Stan said, 'That's for me,' and away they went."

"Come on, Shorty," Father answered him, "let's go see what sort of trouble those two muttonheads have gotten themselves into. I'd like to leave them there to stew awhile, but I guess we'd better get it over with." Turning to the others, he said, "Build up the fire, we might need it."

Off they went. The tracks were easy enough to follow, of course. After about ten minutes or so there were three more shots. Father fired once in answer. They were now on the flat ground of the valley bottom, and in another ten minutes or so they heard voices.

"Take it easy," Father cautioned Shorty. "This is bad ground." He walked carefully, not always following the tracks.

They heard Stan saying loudly, "I can't find anything and my hands are so frozen. I couldn't pick anything up if there was something." His voice sounded strained. They pushed through a bit of snow-covered brush and there he was, standing with his back to them, looking at something below him. He heard them and swung around.

"By God, am I glad to see you!" He was shivering so much he could scarcely get the words out.

"We fell in a hole, that is, Frank did, and I fell in trying to get him out. I got out alright, but he's still in there, and I tried to find a log or something to throw in, but there's too much snow..." He turned away, pointing at something ahead.

They looked to where he was pointing, and saw Frank. Or at least, they saw Frank's head. There was a clear space in the brush. On the side nearest them, the snow was all trampled and muddy. A few paces on was an oval-shaped patch of snow-and-water slush, and in the middle of that was Frank, his chin just level with the surface. He said not a word and his eyes were wild.

Father said, "Funny place to go swimming."

Without waiting for an answer, he told Shorty, "Get Stan back to camp as fast as you can. Keep him moving. I don't care if you have to beat him around the ears with your gun barrel, but don't let him stop."

Turning to Frank, he said, "Don't go away," and then, relenting, "You'll be out of there in a moment."

With admirable calm, Frank answered him, "I'll be here. If I move, I sink deeper. There's rotten branches down there. They won't hold any weight, but if I move my feet, they pull me down."

"I know," said Father.

Moving quickly, he slipped the belt axe out of its thong, and looked around him. They were lucky. There was a tall skinny hemlock tree off to his left.

He went quickly over to it and began to chop. The axe was sharp, the tree no more than four or five inches through. In seconds it was falling toward the pond. He had aimed it to miss Frank's head by about three feet, but from the yell that came from that direction, it must have appeared to be coming right for him.

But it fell true, missing him by an arm's length. Frank needed no urging. He grabbed a branch, pulled himself over to the trunk, and then—for he was a powerful man—heaved himself along it until the ground would take his weight. He stood, dripping water and mud, looking back at the hole. He said solemnly, "I thought I was there to stay. I don't think I'd have lasted another five minutes."

"If you don't get back to the fire pretty soon, we may end up carrying you out of here yet," commented Father, turning to go.

Frank started to follow, then, "Just a minute."

He went a few steps back and to the side, and picked up his gun, which was lying partly buried in the snow where he had thrown it. He slung it over his shoulder by the strap.

"Let's go."

Father looked at him.

"Both your gun and Stan's have slings. They'd stretch about ten feet if they were joined together. Good leather too—take quite a pull."

Frank stopped dead in his tracks. He slipped the gun back off his shoulder, held it by the sling and looked at it.

He said slowly, "Jesus—Christ."

It didn't sound like a prayer.

So now they were all once again gathered around the fire. Frank and Stan were sending up great clouds of steam from their wet clothes, for they had refused to take them off, even to wring them out. They had been back for an hour. It was now about noon. They had about three hours before they would have to make camp again. Four hours until dark, if they tried to press on to the boat. Father thought the margin was too slim. He counselled that they stay there, and start as early as possible next morning. No one argued. In fact no one said much of anything.

Father told me, "You never saw such a downhearted bunch of men as they were when they started out that next morning. I really thought we were in serious trouble. They could barely make it out of camp, and there was at least four hours of hard going ahead of us. But it's funny what a difference a little thing can make in a situation like that.

"A squirrel chattered from the top of one of the trees. It's not uncommon for them to come out for a look around, even in the middle of winter, and this was still early. But no one expected it, and everyone perked up his ears at the sound of it.

"Stan said, 'Meat—is meat. Stand back. He's all mine.'

"He dropped his pack, jacked a shell into his gun and stood ready. They were all looking up into the tree, as serious as if it had been a deer or bear lurking up there in the treetop.

"The schoolteacher spotted it first. He whispered, 'There it is, I see it!' and pointed to a spot right above us.

"Stan stepped back, raised his gun and fired. He was a big man and he had a big gun. I think it was a .44 Winchester. Something like that. Shell as big as a man's thumb. He was a good shot, and he hit what he was aiming at. There was a sort of explosion up in the treetop, and a squirrel's tail came drifting down and lit right in front of us on the snow. Nothing else. Stan went over and picked it up, and when they saw the look on his face everyone started to roar with laughter. They couldn't stop. You know how catching it is when everyone is laughing. I even had to join in myself, and I didn't really think it was all that funny! But the thing is, it perked everyone right up. They acted like new men, and they walked like they had gotten new energy. And what's more, it stayed with them. That squirrel was as good as a meal to those men. Tough on the squirrel perhaps, but I guess at that, it was better than being eaten alive by a hawk or a marten, which is nature's way."

So Father led the way down the valley, and then Shorty, and after him, each of the others took a turn at breaking trail in the snow.

If this was fiction, the last day would be marked by some noteworthy event to cap it all. But life is not always alert to dramatic opportunity, and the day was uneventful. Before dark, they reached the beach, and there was the boat, anchored out on the quiet water of the Inlet.

"The skiff would only hold two," said Father. "I went out to the boat with Shorty, and then sent him to get the others. I lit the fire in the stove. The wood was dry and the stove-top would be red hot in a few minutes. I got my biggest pot and half filled it with water. About two gallons. Then I dumped in a whole bag of rice, and a whole package of raisins. This all took about five minutes. By the time Shorty had the men on board, the pot was starting to steam. It was the fastest and most filling meal I could think of. Now mind you, I wasn't hungry myself. I hadn't felt hungry after the second day. Seven days without food seems rather a long time, but as long as you're not worrying about it, you can do without. But as I was getting things ready, I noticed a dry slice of bread that had been left on the table, so I picked it up and took a bite. And as I started to chew on it, suddenly my mouth filled with saliva, and I was starving hungry, just like that! Just the one little taste of food made my stomach remember what it was there for. You see, after that second day, I had put the idea of eating out of my mind so completely, that I didn't even miss it. But the others, they thought of food, they talked of food, and they kept nibbling leaves and berries, and the result was they were hungry all the time."

(Well, it might have worked for Father, but as a general prescription against hunger, I doubt it would be of much value. However, I record it as it was told to me.)

He continued. "Those men went through that boat like a pack of hungry wolves. Every can, every biscuit, every crust. I managed to save the gallon of peaches for the rice pudding, and when that was finally ready, they tore into it. You wouldn't believe how much rice pudding a man can eat when he puts his mind to it!

"By then, of course, we were heading down the Inlet for home. But they just couldn't leave that rice pudding alone. On the way back they kept dipping out a spoonful now and then until the pot was empty—when they were awake, that is. With their bellies full, and in that warm cabin, they all slept most of the way back. It was about an eight-hour trip, mostly at night, and the sea was dead calm, and I must admit that I came as close to falling asleep at the wheel that night as I ever did."

At last, around midnight, a couple of dim lights ahead showed that they were approaching Egmont. Everyone started to gather up their coats, shoes, guns and so on.

Shorty picked up Father's coat and started to hand it to him. Something fell out of the pocket. He picked it up, looked at it. It was the other chocolate bar. Everyone stopped what they were doing and looked at it and then at Father.

Shorty said incredulously, "You had this in your pocket all the time, and never ate it?"

"Well," said Father, "I was saving it for an emergency."

"It took a lot to get to Shorty," Father told me, "but that was too much. He kept saying to himself, 'An emergency. He was saving it for an emergency!'"

The others didn't say a word, but they looked at him as if he wasn't altogether human.

A bit later, Frank spoke up.

"You know, fellows, our mistake was in leaving it too late. We should have started a bit earlier. Next year..."

"Next year," Stan said grimly, "about this time, or earlier, if someone says the words 'Big Horn,' or 'Sheep' to me, if he doesn't duck quick enough, he won't be able to hold a gun until the hunting season is over. And if I hear of 'living off the land', well..."

His partner decided not to continue.

"And that," said Father, "is the story of the great expedition after mountain sheep. I never heard that anyone ever tried again, and I still don't know if there are any sheep up there."

tꞑe stoics

These days it's not fashionable in fashionable society, to be stoic. A "stiff upper lip" and the desirability of keeping your troubles to yourself are frowned upon. We are counselled to "let it all hang out." A good prescription for getting parts of it cut off! I must confess a preference for the days when "sensitivity" was for poets and well-bred young ladies.

The quality I speak of here is essentially male, nurtured of necessity by warrior societies. Women have a determined tenacity in the face of pain and adversity that is at least as strong as any we males may summon, but it is expressed differently.

So the following stories are about men, for the quiet suffering of their opposites is neither as easy to observe, nor as overtly easy in the telling. It is, I think, essentially male to be flippant in the face of pain or misfortune. I offer the following as an example. It may be apocryphal, though I was assured it really happened.

It was at the cut-off saw in a small sawmill. Such work was fast and dangerous. The operator's foot slipped in the sawdust, he lost his hand, cut off at the wrist. Someone saw, blew the whistle, the mill stopped. The first-aid man came running. While he was working to stop the bleeding, the injured man reached to where the severed hand still lay on the cut-off table.

Picking it up, he offered it to the other, saying "Here, let me give you a hand."

Father's first encounter with this sort of thing was when he was still very young, on one of his first jobs. His boss was a tough and wiry middle-aged logger named Scotty Lyons.

"He was a good man to work with," remembered Father, "but you soon learned you had best not mention anything about being cold, or wet, or tired. If someone new on the job did, Scotty would look at him with those grey eyes, and say, 'Well son, it's nice and warm in the bunkhouse. If you go, just don't bother to come back.' And the tone of his voice would just shrink a man down to about half size. But when you got to know him, you'd walk right off a cliff for him if he asked you to."

They were moving a heavy steam-donkey across the hillside to another location. It was on a big sled, logs five or six feet through. The stumps they used to anchor the line kept pulling out. Scotty was standing on the downhill side of the sled giving orders. He had just set up a pull using two stumps in line, and gave the engineer the signal to go ahead easy. It went pretty smoothly at first, but the engineer was watching the stumps so closely to see that they didn't start to pull out, that he forgot to watch the line on the drum, and it piled up on one side, something that he should have prevented. When it had piled up two or three turns, the top one slipped off and the machine gave a sudden lurch as the line went slack, then another, as it came tight again.

Scotty rode out the first, but the second caught him off balance and he had no choice but to jump down the hill. He went about ten or twelve feet, not enough to do any harm, a few bruises perhaps, no more. Scotty was as agile as a cat, and landed on his feet in perfect balance, but on a sloping log instead of the ground. His sharp caulks held, but Scotty's ankles couldn't. He collapsed in a heap, and got up cursing, but collapsed once again into a sitting position. He stretched his legs out, and the horrified men saw that the soles of his boots were each turned at a right angle to his legs.

He looked at them, then took his right foot in his gnarled and powerful hands and, with a quick jerk, twisted it back into position. There was a loud snap as it went into place. He sat regarding it for a moment, then did the same to the other one.

"Cripes," he said, "I felt that."

He got to his feet and looked up at his crew. "What are you standing around gawking for? We've got a machine to move!"

But even Scotty could only defy nature so far. He began to limp, and then to clutch onto things for support. His normally ruddy complexion became a sickly grey, and sweat streaked his face.

Finally he called a halt. "I'm going to have to find me a bigger pair of boots," he said grimly "—if I can get these ones off."

They had to cut the boots off, and for the first time, Scotty moaned in distress.

"Those were the best boots I ever had," he groaned. "I can't look."

They got the boots off. It must have been agony, although they were made of the softest leather. His ankles were so swollen that the knife-point had to be forced between leather and skin. When it was done, he sat there on the stump looking at his ruined feet.

"Well," he said philosophically, "I guess I'll have to sit out some of the dances next Saturday."

Scotty missed a lot of dances, I'm afraid. The first-aid man took one look and sent him off to the hospital. He was gone for almost a month, and when he did come back, his old sure-footedness was gone; he now limped badly. But he was never heard to complain. That wasn't the sort of thing he did.

The next story I have read several times elsewhere in one form or another. Because of the nature of the work, and the type of man it attracted, it may even have happened more than once. But this one, I am convinced, is authentic.

The high lead—the use of a tall tree, or spar, to keep the head end of the logs off the ground as they were being hauled in—was at that time the preferred logging method. The men who trimmed and topped the trees, the high-riggers, were the new elite of the camps. It was a difficult and dangerous job, and it attracted men who might legitimately be termed "daredevils."

Father tried his hand at it; he thought it looked like fun. It was, to an extent, but he gave it up nonetheless.

He told me, "You had to be able to forget about aches and pains, to not care about getting hurt. You had to be a little bit crazy to enjoy it. I didn't have enough meat on my bones. I was always getting my shins bruised and hurt, and I didn't like it. Couldn't get used to it. The limbs when they let go, would bang you on the feet or shins. The rigging would swing down and bruise you, or the wire would have jaggers to stick you. My hands were always sore. And the belt hurt my ribs from leaning back in it. There was always something ready to get you. It's too bad though. There's no other job quite like it."

Father didn't see this story happen, he was doing the booming work for the outfit at the time. But it was the talk of the camp for a long while afterward. He heard various accounts, and asked many questions, for he knew it was not only a story worth the telling, but one that would be told in as many versions as there might be people telling it.

The high-rigger—or more commonly, just "rigger"— in camp at the time was a feisty little Irishman known as Paddy. Deep-chested, powerful arms, tough as boot leather. In the contests and feats of strength or skill that often took place in bunkhouses to enliven the time between supper and lights-out, Paddy had a trick that no one else was ever able to duplicate. Not even Father, who was good at this sort of thing, and who had one of his own that few others could do.

Paddy called his the "Salmon Flip." Lying with his stomach on the floor, arms straight out from his shoulders, he could contract his muscles violently enough to flip himself off the floor and clap his hands together underneath his body while still in the air, before he hit the floor again! This without using arms or legs to assist him. It was his only trick, but it was a good one.

This day they had moved the big yarding donkey to a new "setting," which meant a new tree had to be climbed, and "rigged" with the guy lines, cables, blocks and so on. Paddy had spent most of the morning trimming off the branches. The tree was standing off by itself, and there were a lot of thick branches, many more than on a tree that is surrounded by others, for shade is nature's pruning method. So he was probably a bit tired when he finally reached the top, a hundred and forty feet up. After he topped a tree, it was Paddy's custom—and that of most others like him—to sit there admiring the view while he had a cigarette and a bit of rest. But this time something went wrong. The men working around the machine heard the cry, "'Ware below!" the warning that something was falling. They looked up to see Paddy hurtling through the air, back to the ground, legs drawn up, arms up and still holding his safety rope. Above him his hat was following him, but more slowly. He hit the pile of branches with a shattering crash,

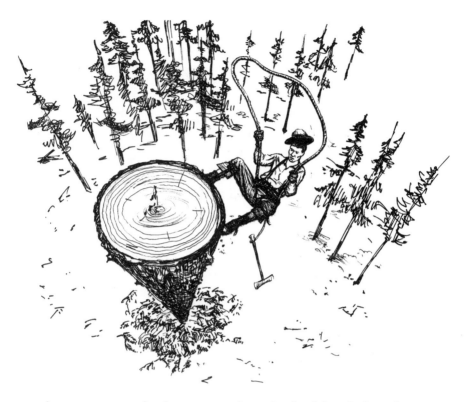

and everyone rushed over to where he had landed and began to pull away the big branches so they could reach him, or rather, his body. But they heard cursing, and the sounds of branches snapping.

"Paddy!" they called. "Are you all right, Paddy? Wait there, we'll get you out."

But Paddy wasn't waiting. Out he crawled, red-faced and furious.

"Can't find m'hat," he snarled. Someone spotted his hat up on the pile of branches and brought it down for him.

"What happened?"

"How'd you come to fall?"

"Did you cut your rope?"

"Are you hurt bad?"

He flipped his rope so it hung over his shoulder and down his back in a loop.

"Only a greenhorn cuts his rope," he said contemptuously. He pushed through them and limped to where his jacket lay on a stump and rummaged through the pockets.

"Forgot m'smokes," he explained.

"Aw, come on, Paddy, what happened up there?"

He took his time lighting a cigarette, limped back and stood there looking at them as they waited for him to speak.

"Well," he said at last, poker-faced, "it was this way. Some horse's-ass cut the top of the tree off, an' I was so busy climbin' I didn't notice it. Got ten feet up in the air before I realized, and then there was nothin' to grab. Hell of a note!"

Everybody laughed, mostly from relief. That was the Paddy they knew! Someone stepped over for a closer look at his back and exclaimed, "Hey, Paddy, you've got a piece of branch stuck in your back!"

"Yeah," he drawled. "I noticed. Pull it out, will ya?"

The man tugged at it tentatively.

"Go on, pull it out. It won't bite you. What are you afraid of?"

They all clustered around for a look. His shirt was torn, showing a long red gash in the white skin. Below it, and in several other places, the cloth was soaked with blood. A hand's-breadth below the left shoulder, a piece of branch the size of a man's finger and about as long, stuck out at an angle. The man withdrew his hand, shook his head.

"I can't do it," he stated positively. Paddy looked around in scorn.

"Is there anybody here that ain't chicken? Never mind, I'll do it m'self."

He groped behind his back, but the hooktender said, "Here, I'll pull it out."

He jerked it free, and blood oozed from the hole.

"Thanks," said Paddy, and began to pick his way through the pile of branches to the tree.

The hooktender, who was in charge of the crew, protested. "You can't go back up there after a fall like that, the shape your back is in. You better go back to camp and let the first-aid man have a look at you."

"Bugger the first-aid man," said Paddy. "I've got a tree to rig!" And back up the tree he went; not as fast as usual perhaps, but surely, and he stayed up there until quitting time.

When they got back to camp that evening, Paddy waved off the first-aid man, went straight to his bunk, pulled off his boots and curled up, clothes still on, face to the wall. He indicated that he didn't want to be called for the evening meal, and went to sleep.

Next morning, he was up in time for breakfast. He stretched gingerly, winced, and said to Father, who slept in the same bunkhouse, "Hal, will you take your knife and cut this shirt off?" As Father began, he added, "Leave the places where it's stuck to the skin. Just cut around them. Best bandage in the world, wool and caked blood. Pulls a bit, but you get used to that. Be as good as new when I put a new shirt on."

"I never," said Father, "saw a back that looked like
that. The whole thing was either bruise or caked blood.
I don't know what the rest of him looked like, but the
bruises didn't stop at his belt. He pulled on a new shirt
and went for breakfast. Wouldn't let the first-aid man
near him. Went off to work, same as usual. Didn't
move his arms and shoulders much, but they said he
finished rigging the tree all that day and most of the
next. I don't know how he did it. That's brutal work for
a healthy man. He healed up all right, good as new in
a week or so. Not a word of complaint from him. But
they say he didn't laugh or joke much that first day!"

Father, Martin Warnock, and a half a dozen or so other
men were lounging about on the veranda of the store
at Egmont one evening in late spring. The sun was still
shining, the sea calm, save for a bit of ripple from a
light breeze out of Jervis Inlet. The talk was of hunting, fishing, logging and mutual acquaintances not
present, the usual inexhaustible and ever-interesting
topics when men of that sort gather. They had been
there for about an hour, when Father noticed a black
speck off Egmont Point, a couple of miles off, where
the inlet began. He called the others' attention to it,
and there was a bit of speculation as to who it might
be, but not much. They would know soon enough.
The talk went on.

As the boat drew closer, Martin said, "It's that handlogger from up past Brittain River."

When Martin Warnock spoke that positively, it was a

rash man that would disagree with him, for he knew the lines of every boat in the area, and most of the people. The boat held its course straight toward the float below them, the steady stroke of the oarsman never faltering. When he was near enough, he braked with one oar and stroked with the other, then shipped the oars as the boat swung crossways and came to rest against the float in a perfect landing. The occupant caught the tie-up rail with his left hand, but made no effort to get out onto the float. He sat a moment, bent over slightly, as if he was tired, then with his other hand beckoned to the men on the veranda.

"Who does he think he is, waving at us like that?" said someone, indignantly.

The man in the boat waited a moment, then waved again.

"He's got some nerve, expecting us to go down there. Comes of living alone like that, I guess," commented another.

But Father had been looking more closely, and something about it bothered him. "I think something's wrong with him. I'm going down to have a look." He rose and went lightly down the stairs from the veranda.

Martin was right behind him, and of course the others must follow, though one of them commented, "Can't be much wrong with him if he can row like that."

As they neared the end of the float several things drew their attention. Most immediately, the bottom of the rowboat had a couple of inches of water in it, the colour of blood. The seat on which the man sat calmly, watching them approach, was smeared and streaked with blood, and on the stern seat lay part of a human leg, still in its boot. And they saw that the man's left leg was missing from a few inches above the knee, where the stump was tied off with a couple of turns of heavy cord. As they stood there staring, speechless, the man spoke. He had a bit of an accent, not much. Polish perhaps, or Finn, Father thought.

"I wonder if I could get someone to run me to the hospital? I did not think I could make it there before dark, and I might not find the way in the dark." And, mistaking the cause of their silence, he reached into his pocket. "I have money; I will pay."

"Put away your money," said Martin gruffly. "What kind of men do you think we are?"

Father said, "I'll take him, he'll be more comfortable. We can throw a couple of the bunk mattresses on the deck for him to lie on."

The man spoke in the same quiet manner. "I don't want to be any trouble. I can just stay here and tow along behind you."

But Father told him, "Don't worry about the trouble. We'll handle that. Just rest easy, we'll have you on deck in a jiffy. I can make better time without your boat behind me." He ran to get his boat ready, while Martin jumped in the rowboat and took it around the float and alongside Father's boat. But the injured man refused to get on the mattresses.

"No sense in getting them all bloody," he protested. Father, to humour him, spread a piece of canvas over them, and the man—refusing help—swung himself over on his big callused hands and lay back with a long sigh.

Then he thrust himself up again. "Bring the leg," he said. So Martin held the leg up to Father, who took it gingerly.

"That was a strange feeling," he said to me, "to hold a man's leg while he sits there a few feet away. I'm not squeamish, mind you, but I didn't like that at all."

They set out for St. Mary's Hospital with all the speed Father could coax out of the engine. He steered from the outside wheel. Martin and another sat on deck.

When they were underway, the man said hesitantly, "If you had some water... I'm very thirsty. I lost a bit of blood. I guess that's why." Handing the wheel over to Martin, Father brought water, and the man drank deeply, and then again. He put the container down and sighed.

"What happened?" asked Father.

"I was on the wrong side of the jack when the log started to go. I tried to run but the jack-handle hit me on the knee, and knocked me down, and the log ran over my leg. When it stopped, I couldn't set the jack, but I could reach my axe. There wasn't much left to cut anyway. But it was good that I had the axe. I would not like to have had to use the pocket knife."

"You mean you chopped your own leg off?" said the third man, aghast.

"It was better than lying there to die."

"But how did you get your leg, if it was pinned?" Father wanted to know.

"Oh, once I was free, I could set the jack then."

Father thought of him crawling around, getting the jack in where it would take the log's weight, no easy job at the best of times, and then heaving on the handle of the jack, with only one leg for support, and weak from shock and loss of blood. He wondered if he could have done it.

("I would have left it there," he told me.)

"That's a forty-mile trip," said Martin, shaking his head in admiration.

"It's hard to row with one leg only," admitted the other. "It throws your balance off, and your side gets sore."

No one spoke for a while, each lost in his own thoughts. When next they looked, the man was asleep.

At the hospital, they got a stretcher to carry him on, and he had to have his leg on it with him. They left him to the competent care of the staff, and went on their way.

Father knew the husband of one of the nurses there, and got the rest of the story from him a few days later, for he was interested in what had happened to the iron-willed handlogger.

The injured man had watched for a few minutes as they cleaned and examined his wound, then he spoke.

"Doctor, I brought the rest of it with me. I thought maybe, I hoped that . . . Doctor, can you sew it back on? Even if it didn't work very well . . . "

The doctor thought he was attempting some sort of macabre joke at first, but then he realized that the man was serious. He explained that, not only was it not possible, but that if they tried, the living part would be infected, and he would die a very painful death.

"Are you sure, Doctor? Not even the slightest chance? I would try. I would like to try, if you would do it." The doctor explained as kindly as he could that it was out of the question; that it would be a serious violation of medical ethics. The injured man looked up at him, and the light of hope in his eyes gradually faded. One of the nurses was crying silently.

The doctor tried to comfort him. "You're a very lucky man, you know, and a very tough one. It's a miracle you're alive, and as for being able to lie there and talk, if I didn't see it I wouldn't believe it for a minute! A very lucky man."

But they could see that something vital had gone from the man, as he said very quietly, "A one-legged man wouldn't be much good as a handlogger. Or anything else I would want to do. Perhaps to beg on the streets, eh, Doctor?"

They put him in a bed, fussed over him a bit, made him as comfortable as they could. After a while, the nurse came, and asked him if there was anything she could bring him. He requested some writing paper and a pencil, which she brought him. He was sleeping when she next came by. When she checked in the morning, he was dead. By his pillow was a hand-drawn cheque for a few hundred dollars, made out to the hospital, and signed. With it was a note, neatly printed. It explained that he had no relations, and wanted the hospital to have his money. It also requested that his boat and his tools be given to the man who brought him to the hospital.

"He willed himself to die," stated Father. "Some people can do that."

I don't remember what Father did with the rowboat,

or if he ever took the tools from where they lay up there among the trees. I doubt it. He might have considered them unlucky, though of course, he was not a superstitious man.

This is another story in which Father wasn't directly involved, but there was a fairly large crew of men there, and over the succeeding weeks, he managed to talk with most of them, so I think the details are probably fairly accurate. The names, however, may not be, as in most of these stories. My memory has supplied some, but in the matter of names, I have no faith in it.

A couple of miles behind the Bloedel, Stewart & Welsh camp at Myrtle Point, Locie #2 was making up a train of cars on the siding and storage area. The first car coupled to the Locie was a box, or covered car. The next two in line were heavy flat cars used mostly for moving equipment. They had the automatic couplers that snapped shut and locked when the cars came together, instead of the hole-and-pin type, which required that someone be there to insert the pin to make the coupling.

When the cars were in position the engineer would get the signal and ease the Locie back until the cars jolted together and the couplings of the first and then the second car were engaged. As there is no give to the solid-iron flat-car frames, this means that the impact on the first car slams it back into the next with terrific force, and with almost no warning.

The day was fine; a gusty west wind had cleared the sky of clouds. The brakeman was attending to something on the third car, near the couplings. A man of middle age, and of long experience, he was well aware of the dictum that you never, for any reason, crossed the track by going between the couplings when the train had steam up.

The engineer got the signal, pulled the whistle cord for a warning, and eased in the throttle. The train moved back almost noiselessly. A gust of wind blew the brakeman's hat off, left it lying on the far track, to be cut in pieces when the train moved. Without thinking, he turned side-on, and stepped quickly through the gap between the couplings to get it. His foot slipped on the track. A spot of dampness perhaps, or a bit of oil or grease on the sole of the shoe. He clutched the coupling to save himself, as the train hit the first car, driving it into the next. Flesh and bone means nothing to a hundred tons of train and load. The couplings, bigger than doubled fists, drove through his body just above belt-level, and locked there. A man nearby, who was looking directly at him when it happened, shouted and waved his arms frantically in the stop signal, but of course, it was far too late. Others saw and came running. Only the engineer knew nothing of what had happened; the boxcar had blocked his view. But he knew that something was wrong. He cut steam, put the brake on and hurried toward the group milling about by the end car. When he saw what had happened, he stopped, stood still for a moment, then approached more slowly. The pinned man was his best friend; they had worked together for years.

The men made way for him as he walked steadily up

to within arm's reach of his friend, and studied the couplings carefully. The injured man was conscious, breathing shallowly. He was slumped forward, holding the coupling bar with both hands, as if to take some of his weight on them. His legs hung limply, without movement. He looked up at his friend and straightened a bit. He spoke weakly at first, but gained strength with every word.

"Well, Clance, I guess they're right. There's no fool like an old fool!"

Clancy shook his head. "I can figure you doin' something stupid, Frank. We all do. But not this sort of stupid!"

Someone said, "For God's sake, pull the release. Get him out of there!" and made as if to reach for the release lever. Clancy put out a hand to stop him.

"Don't touch that," he commanded.

To which his friend added, "The moment you unlock the couplings, I'm a dead man. They're the only thing that's keeping my insides together. I know it's got to be done, but I want to hang around a bit more. I've got a few requests to make first, before I leave." He spoke steadily, voice soft but words distinct. This was his moment, and he would live up to it. (I wonder if the choice of words was a deliberate attempt at humour? I like to think so. We'll never know.)

Someone burst out with "Does it hurt much?"

The injured man looked at him in silence for a few seconds. Finally he spoke. "like the man said, only when I laugh."

His face contorted suddenly into a horrible grimace

and they realized that, incredibly, he was laughing, or rather, trying not to.

"I'd like some water, if you wouldn't mind."

Clancy protested, unthinking, "Water's bad if you're hurt in the stomach."

His friend looked at him solemnly. "Clance, if you make me laugh, I'll come back to haunt you. I swear I will."

"Get the water bag from the cab," Clancy ordered one of the bystanders.

When it came, Clancy held it to his friend's lips, but after the first swallow, he refused more.

"It doesn't hurt all that much," he said. "Not as much as you might expect. There's no feeling below the waist. But it's a strange feeling to know you're a dead man. Kind of relaxes you. Nothing matters much."

His tone changed. "Now listen close, Clance."

"I'm listening."

"I owe ten dollars to the shoemaker. Make sure he gets it. He's a good man, he won't send a bill when he hears." He paused, thinking deeply. "Tell my old lady to get married again, soon as she can. The kid needs a father. Tell her it was my last wish. It's important, Clance, don't forget."

"I won't forget," said his friend.

"And, Clance, you might sort of pass the word around. The better sort will feel bad about being too hasty. Let 'em know I'm all for it. She's a good woman, she should have the best."

He paused. The effort had obviously cost him.

A man said, "We've sent the speeder for the doctor.

He should be able to give you a shot of something."

"What's the use in that?" asked the pinned man. He looked and sounded very tired now. "There's no point in stretching this out. I've said what I had to say. Now I'm just keeping everyone from doing their job. Throw the coupling, let's get it over with."

"You sure that's what you want, Frank?" inquired his friend gently.

"No, but it's got to be done, so do it. So long, Clance. So long, fellows. Sorry to be such a bother."

"So long, Frank." Clancy pulled the bar that unlocked the couplings, and they rolled the car back with a bar. Frank made a gasping sound, as his hands dropped limply from the bar. Clancy grasped him by the arms to keep him from falling onto the track, but his friend was dead.

BEAR OIL

O ne day as he was having supper on his boat at the wharf in Pender Harbour, Father heard heavy footsteps coming across the float. The boat rocked violently, and the door was thrown open even more violently. One of his wilder friends had arrived for a visit. Without so much as a hello, he thrust a bit of paper in Father's face. "Here, Hal, take a look at this!" he shouted. His name was Chuck.

"He mostly shouted when he talked," said Father, "but this time he was louder than usual. In the woods he was as quiet as a weasel, but he made up for it when he was talking to people."

Father took the paper. It had been torn from a page of newspaper. He turned it over looking for some reason for the excitement.

"There," roared Chuck, "where it says 'Wanted'."

Father read, "Wanted, bear oil. Will pay fifty dollars

a pint. Will collect anywhere." And a name and address. He looked up.

His friend was bouncing with excitement. "Fifty dollars a pint. Do you know how many pints of oil you can get out of one bear?"

"No," said Father "I can't say as I do"

"Well, neither do I," admitted the other, "but it sure must be a lot. And bears! I bet we can get a dozen bears just out of the head of Jervis alone. There must be a hundred dollars worth of oil in a dozen bears!"

He held his fingers up in front of him and counted slowly. "Now, there's two pints in a quart and four quarts in a gallon. Right?" He lowered his voice reverently. "A hundred gallons...a hundred gallons of bear oil..."

He shook his head slowly. "Do you know how much a hundred gallons would be worth?"

Father said skeptically, "A lot more than anyone is going to pay for bear oil."

Chuck looked hurt. "What do you mean? It says right there on that piece of paper..."

"I don't care what it says on that piece of paper, no one is going to pay that for bear oil!"

But the other's faith in the printed word wasn't to be shaken so easily. "I suppose that means that you won't come in with me?"

"No," said Father, "I think I'll sit this one out. And I think you had better find out a bit more about this fellow before you go boiling down every bear from here to Toba Inlet."

"Hal," said Chuck, "You are going to be very sorry

about this. Don't say to me later on that I never gave you the chance to get rich."

"No, I won't ever say that, and I appreciate it very much. But I think I'll leave it all to you, thanks just the same."

And so they parted, after Father had promised solemnly "Not to breathe a word of it to anyone."

He did wish he could warn the bears of their danger. His friend was a deadly hunter. People said that he was half animal himself, and it was true that he could certainly think like one. The bears were in for a very hard time!

The days went by, and the weeks, and Father saw no more of the bear hunter. A man of sudden enthusiasms, he had probably gone off chasing some other wild scheme to get rich without going to work. But Father was wrong.

One day, on picking up his mail at the post office, he found a letter from Vancouver. In it, a Mr. Ramsay stated that he would like to hire Father to take him into Jervis Inlet on a certain date, to visit a Mr. D—, the name of the would-be bear-oil tycoon! He had been informed that Father knew where to go and had the means to get there. Sincerely...etc.

So Father posted a short note saying that he would be at the Pender Harbour dock at the suggested date.

Sure enough, at the appointed time, down the gangplank of the Union steamship came someone who, said Father, "looked so out of place there that he could only be the sort of man who would want to corner the market on bear oil." About average height, he was so fat he looked short. He jiggled when he walked, and the gangplank swayed as he bounced down it. He wore a yellow checked jacket in the latest fashion.

"Bright enough," said Father, "to make your eyes water. And green pants. I had never seen green pants before. I decided that I wouldn't mind if I never saw any again."

He went over to this apparition, who was standing looking about him with an air of great interest. "Are you Mr. Ramsay, by any chance?"

"That I am, sir. That I am. That's my name. And you, sir, I assume are Mr. Hal Hammond?" Father admitted to this. "Well, sir, let us be on our way to the place where Mr. D— processes the oil. I am eager to see it. I must admit that I am somewhat incredulous. I have never obtained as much oil as he claims to have, in one place before. How many people does he have collecting for him?"

When Father stated that he was almost certainly working on his own, not being the sort of man to employ others, the fat man stopped in his tracks.

"Impossible," he puffed indignantly.

But Father assured him that Chuck was a noted hunter, and a very hard worker.

"Which he was, when he wanted to be," said Father.

"Though that was not very often."

But at least it seemed to reassure the fat man, although he remained dubious, and kept muttering under his breath, "Impossible, impossible!"

Eventually, after much puffing and blowing, Mr. Ramsay was installed—more or less comfortably—in the cabin of the boat, and they began the long journey to Chuck's shack in Jervis Inlet.

After a time, when they had become somewhat acquainted, and he thought it was discreet to do so, Father inquired casually whether it was really true that Mr. Ramsay was paying fifty dollars a pint for bear oil.

"Indeed, sir, indeed. The demand far exceeds the supply. Even this quantity will only satisfy the market for a few months. It is valued greatly by the Oriental race, sir, as a medicine of great virtue. And many other uses, sir, many other uses."

"I could have kicked myself," remembered Father. "I thought of how Chuck had practically begged me to go with him, of how much bear oil we could have collected. I was making pretty good money, but fifty dollars was a lot in those days. A month's wages for most people.

"Well, we turned the last point, and there was the shack. Chuck had heard the boat and was down on the beach to meet us. His grin was a mile wide. On the front wall, the long one, there were two bear hides stretched out to dry, and when we pulled closer, I could see another one nailed up on the end wall. There were no more showing anywhere else."

Mr. Ramsay was again incredulous. "Is this all? This can't be all there is," he huffed crossly. "I mean, for all that much oil, there should be more."

Father managed—with great difficulty—to get him into the skiff, which was fortunately wide and stable, for there was no dock. Chuck's boat was kept anchored in the bay and visitors had to row to the beach or stay aboard.

He was shouting before they were halfway to shore. "You're late!" he yelled, as if they were a hundred yards off. "I've been waiting for a week for you to show up. But that's alright, gave me time to get some more. I bet I got more bear oil than ever was in one place before!"

At that, Mr. Ramsay brightened noticeably. When the bow of the skiff touched the beach, the fat man scrambled out, completely oblivious of damage to his patent leather shoes caused by the rocks and mud.

"Well," he puffed, "let's see this oil of yours. I trust, sir, that it is of good quality. My customers, sir, expect the best, and that is what I give them."

"Quality," shouted Chuck, "why, I have the best quality bear oil you ever saw in your life!"

They reached the door. He flung it open with a flourish, and waved them by. "How do you like that?" he roared.

Father said, "I looked around. I never saw anything like it. I don't know where he found all those jugs and jars. They covered every flat surface: floor, table, chairs, shelves. And they were all full of yellow oil. Some of them had solid white fat on top. The air was thick with the smell of boiled bear. I decided I wouldn't go on any bear hunts up Jervis Inlet for a while!"

The fat man took one look around and hissed like a

steaming kettle. He bent over, wheezing, and stuck one finger in the nearest jar. He smelled it.

"I thought," said Father, "that he was going to burst. His face turned almost purple. He tried to say something, but he couldn't get it out. He shook his oily finger at us and you never saw anyone so mad in all your life. Finally he managed to speak, but he sounded as if someone was choking him."

"Bear oil! Bear oil! You fool," he screamed, "this is not bear oil, it's bear *fat*! Do you hear me? Bear *fat*! You've got me all the way up here to show me *bear fat*!"

"But what's the difference?" protested his victim, his aggrieved voice plaintive and less loud than Father had ever heard before. "Bear oil, bear fat, it's all the same thing, isn't it?"

The fat man said bitterly, "If you weren't so stupid, you would be pitiful. I'll tell you what the difference is. You shoot your bear. You cut off its paws. You cut slits in the fingers and hang them in a cool place. Out of the slits drips a clear fine oil. You get about a tablespoon to each paw. That's bear oil. That's what I came to this godforsaken place to get. *And you haven't got any!!*"

He turned to go, shaking his head in fury. Chuck said faintly, "Wait a minute . . . " then with more strength, "Wait a minute." The fat man turned impatiently. "Well, what is it?"

Chuck said truculently, "What about all this oil here? It must be worth something. I'll let you have it real cheap. The people who buy from you probably wouldn't know the difference anyhow."

The fat man turned to Father in disbelief, "Give him

for it? Give him for it?" He swung on Father's friend. His tone cut like a sharp knife. "If I thought you had enough brains sir, to make any money, I would demand that you pay for my wasted time and the cost of my journey. But I do not believe, sir, that you have as much brains as one of those bears that you have so wantonly shot. As to your *bear fat*, you may drown yourself in it, sir, and good riddance!"

He turned toward the door. Father looked at his friend, and tried to think of something to say. He couldn't. Chuck's face was brick red. Suddenly he took a couple of quick steps to the stove, where there was a small washtub full of bear oil. He picked it up by the handles and stepped quickly toward the door. "Hold on there!" he called.

The fat man had stopped in the doorway and was turning to see if Father was following. He received the entire tub of bear fat on his head, checked coat and green trousers.

Chuck said quite gently, "There, you can take that back with you. You can have it for nothing. Best Jervis Inlet bear oil."

Then he roared with a voice that made the windows rattle. "And if you're not out of here in one minute, I'll boil you down and see what kind of oil all that blubber will make!"

Mr. Ramsay had been standing frozen with shock and horror after his oily bath.

"Fortunately," said Father, "the oil was just warm, so he wasn't scalded. But he turned and went down that beach like the scalded cat in the old saying. I never saw anyone so fat move so fast."

Father turned to go. His friend said after him, in a voice hoarse with intensity, "Get him out of here. If you don't get him out of here quick, I'll kill him. I swear it."

Father got him out of there, fast. He said, "I never again said the words 'bear oil' to Chuck, in fact, I was a bit leery of saying the word 'bear' to him! I didn't think it would be a very good idea. I often wondered what he did with all that bear grease. He was a man who didn't like to waste anything!"

SVENÐSON
AND ThE
TAXMAN

F ather was working on his boat at the dock in
Pender Harbour. This wasn't at all unusual. The
owner of an old wooden boat, if he wishes, can
spend most of his spare time at this, and Father was
fussy about maintenance. The year, probably 1919.
Perhaps 1920.

The *Cassiar* had docked and was loading freight
and passengers. Immersed in his repair job, he paid
little attention until there came the hard sounds of
leather soles on wood. He looked around to see a
stranger approach and stop. A cadaverous-looking
man, middle aged, neatly dressed in dark suit and

darker tie, a raincoat folded over his left arm. He wore severe rimless glasses and peered through them at the young man rather as if he was examining a bug that was new to him.

"Are you Mr. Hal Hammond?" he asked, in a soft smooth voice.

Father said thoughtfully, "It could be two men you're looking for. One of them's known as Hal; then there's a Mr. Hammond . . . "

The man regarded him with an icy stare. "You were pointed out to me as being Mr. Hal Hammond. Now, what kind of foolishness are you up to? Are you, or are you not, he?"

"You look like a government official to me," said Father coolly. "A lawyer friend of mine told me never to admit anything to government officials. But just supposing I was this Hal Hammond, what would you be wanting him for?"

"Lawyers!" sniffed the other contemptuously. "A useful tool but they need watching. As to why I am here, I need transportation and I was told that you could supply it."

"I think," said Father cautiously, "that could be arranged. Just where do you want to go?"

"There is a man called Svendson, who operates, I believe, a logging camp somewhere in the vicinity. I wish to see him on government business. Do you know his whereabouts?"

"I know Svendson. He has a camp up in the inlet. I can take you . . . Take about two hours to get there, though."

Time seemed no worry to the stranger. He agreed readily to the fee, and before long, they were heading up the channel toward Jervis Inlet.

When some time had passed in silence, Father tried a few conversational gambits. They produced only the minimum response. But then the other produced one of his own. "This Svendson, does he have a profitable business?"

Father considered this, and answered that he really couldn't say.

After a few more tries, the man tried another tack. "A nice boat you have here. Does it bring you much income?

Some instinct of self-defence stirred in Father's mind, as he hedged, "Oh, I make just enough to pay for fuel and repairs."

The stranger looked dubious. "Then it would not appear to be worthwhile to do it, if that's the case."

"No," agreed Father blandly, "probably not worth-while. But it's a living."

There was a long silence as the man turned this over in his mind a few times. His long face assumed the expression of one who has found something in his soup, but hasn't quite decided to call the waiter. He sat there silently, and Father made no more attempts to communicate, so the rest of the trip was made in silence.

At last, Svendson's A-frame came into view, and Father steered in toward it. An A-frame consists of a couple of long trees, usually on a float. They are tied together at the top, but spread wide on the float to give stability. Cross braces make it look more or less like an *A*, and support wires—guy lines—hold it upright. A heavy wire goes from a machine on the float through a pulley at the peak of the *A* and up the sidehill into the woods. Much of the steeper parts of the coast were logged in this way. They can be quite efficient. Svendson's was not one of these.

There was no sign of activity as they eased into the float alongside Svendson's old boat, but as he was tying up, Father saw the man they were looking for appear out of the shed that held the machine. He came across the logs to greet them, wiping his hands on his clothes as he came. Of average build, he was balding, but made up for that with an unusually thick moustache. He wore the usual caulk boots and heavy pants with wide braces, but no shirt, only the gray Stanfield underwear worn by almost all loggers. This was almost as much hole as cloth, and out of the holes on his chest stuck tufts of hair of the same light brown as that on his lip and scalp. There was black grease smeared on his head and face, and two broad strips of it on his chest where he wiped his hands.

"Hello, Hal." He put out blackened hands. "Guess what I've been doing? Machine's down again." Looking at the man in the expensive suit, "Who's your friend? I'm afraid I'm not hiring at the moment." His eyes twinkled as he almost grinned.

Father, out of his passenger's line of sight, rolled his eyes and shrugged his shoulders eloquently, as the man made his way carefully across the deck of Svendson's boat and onto the big logs of the A-frame float.

Safely there, he said with some dignity, "I assume you are Mr. Svendson? I am not applying for employment, sir. My name is Turner." He held out his hand, but on seeing the state of Svendson's, withdrew his protectively to his pocket. "I represent the Government of Canada. To be more specific, the Income Tax Department."

(Income tax had been imposed in 1917 as a war-time measure, with the assurance that it was only temporary. It is said that people actually believed this!)

Svendson withdrew the proffered hand.

"Income tax? What do you mean, income tax?"

"You should know, Mr. Svendson, as a businessman, that you, and all people earning over a certain amount of income, are required to pay a tax on it, as of 1917."

"Ay be not busynessman, ay be logger. Ay make no money, ay pay no tax." Svendson had suddenly acquired an accent. As Father well knew, this was a device of his that allowed him to misunderstand whenever he chose, and thus give him time to think. He had honed it to a fine point on persistent creditors.

The taxman said patiently, "That may be so, Mr. Svendson, but you must file the papers to prove it. There are no papers filed by you since the tax was imposed. None at all."

Svendson shook his head. "Ay file saws. Ay not file paper. Vat do you mean, file paper?" He squinted his eyes and pursed his lips, which made him look like a caricature Swede.

"Mr. Svendson, I must remind you that this is a serious matter. I am here to audit your books, and to determine how much money you owe the government. Now, show me your office, and we can begin."

"Office?" countered the Swede. "Vot do you tink I am, a doctor? Dere is no office, no books—unless you vant my girlie magazine—and I owe the government notting! Vat has de government done for me, that I should give dem money? Vill you tell me dat, Mr. Government man?"

"Why, there is the army to maintain, for one thing. A war is very expensive you know."

"De var is over. For vy do ve need an army? Und dey said de tax vas only till de var vas over."

"Well," said the other firmly, "I'm afraid it's going to last a bit longer. The government needs money to help the country become prosperous. And there's the police, the mail service, the roads..."

187

"I saw a policeman vunce," mused Svendson, "at a dance. He was drunk. I haf no car, and for de mail, I buy stamps. Und, if de government takes people's money, how can dey be prosperous?"

"But you may want to buy a car, and then there will be roads to drive on."

"Den I vill pay de gas tax, vot is for to build de roads."

By this time, the accountant having forgotten his original purpose, was now determined to justify his employers. He said earnestly, "Mr. Svendson, you must realize, that running a country costs a great deal of money. There are construction works: the parliament buildings, for example. There are a great many government employees that must be paid. People must pay taxes, Mr. Svendson."

But Svendson was having none of it. "By Yeesus, you are right about costing money! Vat do dey need big rock houses for to sit in anyhow. And dere's a lot too many people vorking for de government should have an honest job, instead of going around bothering oder people vot are trying to earn a living."

This rather low blow had its effect. His opponent flushed, and went on the attack.

"People must pay taxes," he insisted hotly. "You can't just take from the country, Mr. Svendson, you must also give something to it."

But Svendson was more than ready for this one. "I pay stumpage tax on every tree, Mr. Turner, and yust about everyting I buy, the government's got a finger in it somehow. And as for de country, vy, vere vould it be witout people like me? De towing boats get vork, de carpenters vot use de vood get vork. Und nail makers, und hardvare, und everybody. Und vot do I get?" He put a finger in one of the holes in his Stanfields, and out another. "Dese here are my best pair. De other is a bit vorn. And now, ven I make a bit of money to keep, you say dey are going to take some of it away!"

The taxman, obviously taken aback, perhaps as much by the decrepit state of Svendson's underwear as much as by its owner's rebuttal, actually appeared to be sympathetic. "But you should realize, Mr. Svendson, that you are not very likely to have to pay a large amount of tax. In fact, I would estimate that it is not at all likely to exceed ten per cent of your net income. You surely must admit that one dollar out of ten is not very much to give for the running of your country."

"It was the wrong thing to say," laughed Father. "Up until now, the talk had been all sort of theoretical, not real, but now it was down to earth; it was real dollars that were coming out of Svendson's pocket. Out of every ten dollars, he was going to lose one, if the tax-man was right!"

Svendson blinked with shock. He lost every trace of accent as he said in disbelief, "Ten per cent! Ten dollars out of every hundred! Do you mean to stand there and tell me that out of every thousand dollars that I make, they are going to take away one hundred?" As the sums mentioned grew larger, Svendson's voice grew louder, more incredulous.

"Well, not exactly," said the gaunt man in his precise way. "The rate rises with the amount earned . . . " Then, seeing Svendson's face, he added hastily "but there is a tax-free minimum, you know."

But Svendson was considering something, and didn't appear to have heard the last bit. "Do you mean to say, that some big shot banker that makes a million dollars will have to pay more than a hundred thousand dollars of it to the government?"

The accountant actually smiled at such naiveté, an expression that ill-suited his long cadaverous face. "Oh well, Mr. Svendson. We must be realistic about these things. The wealthy have resources that are not available to people like us."

Svendson nodded thoughtfully. "Yes," he murmured. "I thought so. And what will happen Mr. Taxman, if I don't pay these taxes?"

The other man looked shocked at such a heretical notion. "Why, they will seize your goods, all you own. They will take your machine there, and your logs. You could even go to jail!"

Svendson nodded again, appeared to come to some decision. "Wait there," he said, with the air of one who has been relieved of a burden. "I'll be right with you. I just have to call my two men."

He turned and went over to the shed, from which a piercing whistle sounded. A shout from up on the hill replied. There was a slight delay, then he reappeared, carrying a battered suitcase. He was now wearing a shirt. "It'll just be a minute. I have to tell the men what's going on, then I'll be ready to go."

"Go, Mr. Svendson? Where are you going?"

"Why, to jail, of course." He waved his hand comprehensively. "She's all yours. Tell the government they can have it, every bit of it. It's not worth a thing. The engine won't run, the lines are shot and the timber's rotten; I've got no money, so I guess it's jail." He seemed quite cheerful about the prospect, rather like someone heading out on a picnic than otherwise.

"Now, wait a moment, Mr. Svendson. I'm sure you are being too hasty. This isn't at all necessary, you know."

But Svendson had made up his mind. "I want to go to jail," he insisted. "I need a rest." He held out his hands. "I work my fingers till my hair falls out, and what for? So's someone can take the little bit of money I put by."

"But, ten per cent, maybe less, it's not so much to get all excited about."

"Only ten per cent, you say. But just look here, Mr. Taxman. After a working man has paid for all he needs, about all he has left over is ten percent of what he makes, so what you are asking for is really one hundred per cent, and I am not going to pay it!" Svendson's mood had changed. He was now waving his arms and shouting, causing the other to look nervously behind him, making sure of the path back to the boat.

"Take me to jail!" shouted Svendson, red-faced. "I insist you take me to jail. Three meals a day and no worries. A roof that don't leak and no damn engines to break down. I want to go to jail!" By this time the accountant had made his way across the cluttered deck of Svendson's boat to the comparative safety of Father's. He said, low-voiced but urgently, "Hurry, let's get out of here, the man's gone crazy. You don't know what he might do. Hurry up, he may come after us!"

Svendson was now on the deck of his boat, still

shouting that he wanted to go to jail, that the government could have everything.

"Wait for me," he pleaded, as Father shoved off. But he seemed oddly slow in covering the short distance to Father's boat. Then Father had shoved the clutch in, and they were gliding swiftly away as the boat gathered speed. The taxman's back was turned, and he was staring resolutely down the inlet to where civilization lay. Father looked back to where Svendson was standing on the deck of his boat. He was waving happily, and there was a big grin under the bushy moustache.

The house by the Talking falls

Father was in a mood to reminisce. I had asked him about old buildings and strange people.

"Something that few people know," he began, "is that all along the coast in the early days, there were houses. Some of them in the strangest places, where you'd never expect to find a house. Not just shacks but big houses, two or three storeys, some of them. Of course, in those days, when there might be ten or fifteen kids in a family, you needed a pretty big place if they were all going to live under one roof.

"But things don't always work out the way we think

they will. Most times the kids moved away as soon as they had a chance. Girls usually got married young and their men didn't want to stay there and be bossed around, and the sons went out and got a job someplace. So you'd come across these big places, all run-down, usually with an overgrown orchard back in the woods. There might be an old couple there, desperate for visitors. Mostly there seemed to be one old man. Either his wife had died from loneliness and overwork, or had left him to go and live where there were people. Women need people around them, even if it's just one neighbor a mile away. You see, a man is satisfied to live alone with only his wife and his work for company, but most women need another woman nearby.

"You'd see them sometimes, worn down to bone and leather, and all they had left to show for it was a house falling down around them, and a family that never came back to visit. There were always a few that thrived on it, and were cheerful in spite of it, and their men had a satisfied look about them. But most of them, in the really remote places, either left or died, and the others had eyes that made you uncomfortable to look into. But it was the old men alone by themselves that grew strange. A man isn't meant to grow old like that, without a wife. Women are stronger and more sensible. They'll either cope, or move away if they're left alone. But men are different. They grow strange. Most of the ones I met were a bit odd. Some were downright crazy, and you had to be careful how you handled them. And there were some that nobody visited, ever. Word got around. I always felt sorry for the old fellows; some were pretty decent, and I liked to visit them when I could. Listen to their stories, jolly them up a bit. But the strangest person I ever saw wasn't an old man, but a young woman, and what's more, she lived in the strangest place I ever saw."

I was immediately interested. Most of Father's stories I'd heard before, but this sounded like one that was new to me. I made encouraging noises, and he began.

"It was the spring of 1923. I'd taken some surveyors up to Minstrel Island to leave them at one of the camps. It was way out of my usual territory. The weather was good and I had lots of time, so I decided to come back by way of the Inside Passage, through Sunderland and Cardero Channels. There were lots of places along there, and on the way down to Toba Inlet, that I'd never had time to look into before. So I moseyed along, stopping here and there to look around, and just generally enjoying the scenery.

"I came to a part where the shore wasn't very interesting, just mountains coming right down to the water, with the usual creeks coming out of the usual mountain valleys, and I was kind of thinking of turning back, when I saw a flash of light from up on the shore just ahead. I thought it was probably just a wet rock up there on the bluffs, but then it came again and I made out part of the outline of the roof of a house there in the trees, a few hundred feet back from shore. There were just a few feet of roof, with a window up under the peak and it was the glass that had made the flash. I thought 'Whoever built that, didn't want to be seen easily.' I decided to investigate. If I'd known what I know now, I'd have turned tail and run for home!"

He pulled the clutch into neutral, letting the boat glide slowly to a stop while he considered the situation. He admired how well the builder of the house had managed to conceal it, yet still have an unobstructed view across the water. It was hidden by a rock knoll covered by bushes and scrub trees that rose beside a good-sized mountain stream. Through the trees he could see the white gleam of a waterfall, and behind the house a curved shoulder of mountain, whose bare rock cliffs, streaked with various shades of grey, would serve to hide any smoke which might rise in front of it. To a casual eye, the bank of the creek appeared to rise straight into the mountain, but he knew there must be a bend, and level ground where the house stood. He engaged the clutch and let the boat idle quietly toward the shore, noting as he did so that the triangle of roof had disappeared behind the trees on the knoll.

A hundred feet or so from shore, he brought the boat to a stop and shut off the engine. He listened. The chattering of the creek as it rushed through the broken rock of the shore into the sea and the subdued roar of the falls were the only sounds that disturbed the silence. He noticed suddenly that the flat shape he had taken to be a partly submerged boulder by the creek mouth was actually the weed- and barnacle-encrusted cabin of a sunken boat, of a design much like his own. It made him immediately uneasy, though he saw no reason why he should feel that way. Sunken boats were a common enough sight on the coast. He looked along the rocky shore. There were faint traces of a trail visible to a sharp eye, but no indication that there had ever been a dock or other structure. Deciding to go ashore for a quick look to see if anyone was living there, he went to the bow and threw out the anchor, testing to make sure it was secure. Then, instead of starting the engine, he unshipped the emergency oars, set them between the thole-pins, and took a few strokes toward the shore. It was not, he realized, that it would be more difficult to start the engine, but that he felt a strong reluctance to disturb the silence.

When he judged the distance was right, he shipped the oars, secured the anchor line and slid the skiff over the side into the water. Finally, he tied one end of a coil of rope to a cleat on the stern of the boat for a shore line, and threw the rest into the stern of the skiff. In some things Father was a methodical and careful man, in others he seemed incredibly reckless. But one thing he never took chances with was the safety of his boat. He would never go ashore without tying it as if he was going to be away for days. As he said, "You never knew for sure how long you would be gone, and it might be a long hard walk home." He leaped into the skiff and sculled it ashore with an oar over the stern. Jumping out onto the rocks, he pulled the little boat safely beyond the tide line and tied it to a convenient bush, and the boat's shoreline to a small but sturdy tree. Then he walked a few slow steps up from the water's edge, looking around him carefully.

There was a small canoe half full of water concealed behind a clump of bushes. It had once been red, but most of the paint had flaked off, exposing the cedar strips underneath. Otherwise it was in good condition. He regarded the water in the canoe with approval. Many people turned their boats upside down to keep them dry. Others knew better and let them fill with water to keep the wood from drying out and shrinking.

He walked silently on up the trail until he was about a hundred feet above the water, then stopped for another look around. The trail hadn't been used recently. No apparent effort had ever been made to improve it. It simply followed the contours, making its way around boulders and over ledges in the most direct manner possible. It was quite steep. Carrying the materials up the trail to build a house must have been hard word. He noticed a few big stumps along the left bank of the creek. The trees, almost concealed by bushes, still lay where they had fallen. The A-frame loggers hadn't been along here, for there was no useful timber along the shore, and it would be a long time before the sparse trees in the upper valley would be worth the effort and expense of surmounting the sheer drop over which the falls plunged. He could hear their roar more clearly from here. There was a curious, irregular, almost vocal quality to the sound. He listened for a moment, then gave a mental shrug. All waterfalls talk. This one just talked a bit louder than most. He looked out over the calm water to the surrounding coastline. The only signs that humans existed were a few scars from A-frame logging, rapidly healing. No boats, no houses. The nearest people he knew of were those at a small logging camp on an island about twenty miles away.

As he stood there watching and listening, the quality of light changed perceptibly, and he knew that the sun had set behind the mountains. The far hills were still in sunshine, but the sea before him had turned a darker green. Although there were a couple of hours yet before nightfall, the premonition of it was in the air.

He debated whether to go on or return to the boat, and begin again in the morning with a full day of light ahead of him. Even now it would be gloomy up there among the trees. On the other hand, he thought that sleep would not come easily that night. Someone might have seen or heard his boat, might be watching him from concealment, quite possibly contemplating a midnight visit! The prospect did not appeal to his always active imagination. Better to investigate now. It could well be that he would be welcomed, and might spend a pleasant evening exchanging stories. Just then, ringing clearly through the still air, came the sound of an axe striking wood. So familiar, so 'homey' was the sound, that his apprehensions instantly became ridiculous, and he turned and began to climb briskly up the trail.

He said, "It was such a familiar sound. I never stopped to think that even a homicidal maniac would still need a fire or that the sound meant that he'd have an axe in his hands!"

The way led around to the right of the knoll, and into a dip, or low spot between it and the gradient that led to where the steep cliffs began, then through a strip of bushes, and suddenly, there was the house at the edge of a fairly extensive piece of flat ground. He could see it plainly, for the bushes and small trees had all been cleared away. The wood chopper was working about eighty feet away, in full view, back turned toward him, but it was the house that held his first fascinated attention.

He told me, "Of all the crazy places to build a house I've ever seen, that one takes the cake. Whoever built it must have had more than one screw loose. The only thing I could figure was he must have decided exactly where he wanted the lookout window to be, built the house under it, and hang the trouble!"

The edge of the bank was at least a hundred feet above the creek bottom, and from a point just ahead of him, swung in toward the cliff face. There at about the centre—the point where it began to curve out again— it was so steep that the ground had slid into the creek, leaving a stretch of rock slope about seventy or eighty feet wide, too vertical to climb without great difficulty. On this, the house had been built, on slender-appearing posts a full forty feet long. No part of it was on flat ground, the entire building being suspended over the steep drop to the creek bed.

It was huge, by the standards of the time. Three storeys plus the roof peak, each storey large enough for an average family to live in comfortably. He realized that the long posts only appeared slender in relation to the bulk of the house; they were actually quite fair-sized trees, expertly braced and buttressed. It was roofed and walled with split-cedar shakes, probably from the trees whose stumps he saw scattered about the clearing. There were many windows of various sizes, some with panes of ornamental glass. All this he saw in only a few seconds, for the trail here was only a few feet from the edge of the bank and the view was unobstructed. He looked quickly around the area behind the house. Most of the bigger trees had been left standing, but otherwise the ground was open until the undergrowth began once more on the other side of the clearing. No gleam of green showed under the big trees, for the overarching canopy of an old-growth forest steals the life-giving light. But a thousand shades of brown from bark and moss, and rotting wood and needle-covered ground glowed softly in the sheltering gloom.

He saw a small building that he thought was probably a tool shed, and a flat-roofed chicken house, to judge from the birds scratching around it. He saw two goats regarding him with that scornful look that goats have. Somewhere beyond, he heard the unmistakable grunt of a pig. More or less what you might expect to see at isolated dwellings anywhere along the coast. Then at last—his surroundings clearly in his mind—he looked closely at the wood chopper. Whoever it was didn't look very menacing, but he thought it might be best not to startle him.

He called "Hello-o there!" The figure dropped his axe and spun around to face him. But, instead of the ancient curmudgeon he'd been expecting, it was a young woman confronting him! He walked toward her, saying in a natural tone of voice "I hope you don't mind a visitor?"

She in turn had taken a dozen or so steps toward him, and they were now only a few paces apart. She replied hesitantly, her tone a rich contralto, but spoke so quietly he could scarcely hear what she said.

"Visitor? Oh, we never have any visitors." Then, more audibly, "Why would you want to visit us? How did you get here? Where did you come from?"

He thought the questions a bit odd. After all, he must have come by boat, and from where hardly seemed relevant. However, upon seeing her more closely, he was so entranced that he hardly knew what she was saying, for here in this wild and unlikely setting was someone truly exotic. It was not a word Father would have used, but it was the sort of word he was searching for when attempting to describe her.

She was dressed in men's clothing, and seemed to be about eighteen years old, or at most, twenty; slim and yet strong-looking. Her hair was honey-blonde, streaked and marked with darker shades, but instead of the light complexion normal to most blondes, her skin was tawny, almost oriental in colour. But what startled him and made everything else seem almost normal was that her eyes shone with the clear yellow of the eyes of a cat!

"I never saw such eyes in a human face," he said. "They belonged on a cat. I didn't think humans could have eyes that colour. It made me think of some kind of human animal standing there looking at me. I'll never forget those eyes!"

Now, I am well aware that it would accord better with reality if she was depicted as having bad teeth and weighing two hundred pounds; however, reality often treads where—for fear of ridicule—fiction may not go. And here, in this house on the edge of the shadowlands, it seems right that the requirements of normality should be ignored.

He didn't remember what he said next, or what she said in reply. What he did remember was her inviting him in for a cup of tea, and that they were chatting away like old friends after a long separation. This may seem unlikely, and I feel that an explanation might be in order, for there is an explanation.

The fact is, Father had a way with women, one that I have never seen evidenced by any other man. It had nothing to do with the ability some men have to ingratiate themselves with, or otherwise impress some females. No, in Father's case it appeared to be due to the fact that he honestly believed women were a finer,

higher sort of being than men. I think that this curious aberration in an otherwise rational man was caused by his devotion, from an early age, to stories of the romanticized Middle Ages of chivalry and knights-errant, and that strange idealization of women that was a feature of a great part of it. Something in this mythos found a home in his mind, and he never rejected it, even in old age. It is difficult to understand how this fantasy could have survived the travails of being raised amongst six sisters, but it did. Perhaps having to leave home at an early age helped! His brother Clifford, exposed to the same influences, and as passionately devoted to the same stories, wasn't able to reconcile them with reality, and as a result became something of a misogynist. But Father, stronger in defence of what he chose to believe, held true to it against all odds.

In some way women seemed to be able, almost instantly, to detect this attitude on first meeting him, and the strange thing is that they seemed to attempt to live up to it. Noted harridans would make him an exception to their hatred of all males, and would bask in the unwonted glow of being esteemed simply for the fact that they were female. I hasten to add, there was nothing sexual in it. Still, the fact that he was a handsome and personable young man with a puckish sense of humour probably did no harm.

So you can see that there was more to this sudden intimacy than simplicity or loneliness on the girl's part. (In fact, she didn't seem lonely at all, but quite content with her life.)

As they walked toward the house, Father inspected it

with much interest. He noticed that it was fairly old. The ends of the shakes were notched and ragged with years of rain. It takes a long time for cedar to weather like that. On the right-hand side of the porch, a little stream gurgled along to tumble over the bank onto the rock. Part of it was channeled into a trough to make a convenient place to fill a water bucket. This side of the house seemed to consist of two fairly large rooms, each with a similar window; two rows of small ornamental panes on top, to let in the light, with one large clear pane below to see through. The one on the left had white lace curtains tightly drawn. In the other, the curtains were pulled back, and, through the glass, though the light was dim, he thought he could see what appeared to be kitchen shelves. There was a door leading into this side.

There was another storey above, with three smaller windows, and one below to which a set of stairs on the left gave access. A chimney of natural stone extended high above the kitchen roof, which must have been supported by heavy beams, since there had been nothing of it showing when he had looked beneath the house. Off to the right, he could see the waterfall through the trees, and part of a long dark pool in the creek below it. Here the sound was quite loud, and again he noticed the peculiar vocal quality to it.

As they stepped onto the porch, there sounded a thunderous roar from the lower storey, so deep and powerful that it seemed to shake the very leaves on the trees! The girl took a couple of steps to the side and called sternly down the stairs, "Quiet, Thunder—it's all

right. Good dog." There was the sound of chain rattling, and querulous dog sounds.

She said, "Don't mind Thunder. He's all right. He
can't get out."

He noted that she didn't say, "He's all right. He
won't hurt you," but simply that he wouldn't have the
opportunity to do so, and filed the information for possible future use.

She opened the door and stood holding it while he
entered, after he had scraped his shoes politely on the
rough boards of the porch. The light in the kitchen
was rather dim, for one of the windows faced into the
trees, and the other toward the mountain, so it took
his eyes a few minutes to adjust. As they did, he saw
a sink and counter under the window facing the
mountain; no taps, just a bucket of water on the
counter near the sink. There was a table and chairs by
the near window, and across from them a big stove, its
pipe leading into the stone chimney. Beside it on the
left was a woodbox, and on that a small tabby cat. A
door on the left led to what was probably a living
room with a fireplace, the only reason one would build
a stone chimney. As far as he could tell in the dim
light, the kitchen was spotlessly clean. He sat in the
chair while she began to make the tea. The cat jumped
down from the woodbox, walked over to him and
rubbed against his leg, purring. The girl said, "Her
name is Tabitha. I think she likes you."

He said, "Hello Tabitha," and stroked its head, and
before long the little cat was settled in his lap. All the
while, the girl had been talking animatedly. She was

very curious about the "world outside" as she called it, and asked a great many questions about it, and the more detailed his answers, the more questions they led to. The rich tone of her voice, the animation of her manner, and the total attention she paid to what he had to say, made talking with her a most pleasant experience. Her name was Mary, but, she explained, her Father had renamed her Melody because of her voice. Father didn't care for either name.

"Someone who looked like that," he explained to me, "should have a name to fit. Something different." He always spoke of her as "the girl with the yellow eyes," or simply "the girl."

The time passed quickly. Tea was served with biscuits and wild blueberry jam. The tea tasted a bit strange, almost bitter, with a hint of some sort of herb. Some blend, he decided, with which he wasn't familiar. It hadn't come from a package, but from a pottery jar she took from the shelf. It was refreshing, and he had another cup. As he sat there, idly swirling the last of the second cup, he noticed some tiny brown globules floating among the tea leaves. Startled and curious, he fished out a couple on the tip of his little finger and asked her, "What are these little seeds?"

"Oh," she answered, "they're from a plant that grows along the creek bank. Great-Gramma showed them to me. We gather them in the fall. They're good for you."

Father was horrified. He was extremely fastidious, even fanatic about something that might affect his faculties. He wouldn't—at that time—touch alcohol, not so much as a glass of beer although he had tasted it and liked it. I think if he had known that ordinary tea itself contained a drug, much as he enjoyed it, he would have forsworn it. So the knowledge that he had just drunk something brewed from the seeds of an unknown plant affected him most unpleasantly. He even wondered if the strange young woman had drugged him for some reason, but then remembered that she had filled her cup from the same pot as his.

(I sometimes wonder if some of the emotions he experienced that night were at least partly due to the effects of that tea, for Father was at all times in complete mastery of his emotions.)

He asked, in a voice that may not have been totally steady, what the seeds did to you. He meant to say "for," but "to" slipped out. She must have noticed his disturbance, for she hastened to reassure him, "Oh, they won't do you any harm at all. They just make you feel good."

As this was exactly what he was afraid of, it failed completely to have the effect intended. But then came the real shock. From over by the stove, a voice like a raven's hoarse croak said harshly, "That's right."

He looked intently at the shadowed wall, expecting to see a parrot, which the voice reminded him of, but what emerged to his incredulous gaze, gradually assumed the figure of an ancient man huddled in the depths of a large chair. The pale face made somewhat shapeless by long straggly grey hair tangling into an even sparser grey beard, had blended perfectly into the shadows on the wall. Father could not believe that he had been in this room for more than an hour and had not detected the presence of another person! His faith in the acuity of his perceptions was severely shaken.

Noticing his shocked look, the girl said brightly, "Oh, that's only Uncle. He says that every once in a while. He doesn't mean anything by it. I don't think he notices what we say." She paused, then, "It's getting pretty dark in here. I'd better light the lamp." As the light brightened, he examined the figure it revealed and half wished the room would regain its sheltering darkness, but hastily repented. It would not be a comforting darkness now, for the figure in the chair was not a reassuring sight. The chair was larger and deeper than it had first seemed. It was made of tree limbs chosen for their shape, over which was draped a bearskin, hair side out. The old man was almost out of sight in it, little more than his feet, legs and head showing. And his hands. Father stared in fascination at those hands. Monstrous hands, with fingers twice the normal length. They were not folded or relaxed, but crouched there on the long bony thighs like huge pale spiders ready to pounce!

Not liking the trend of his thoughts, he wrenched his eyes from the hands to examine the face, which was turned slightly into the room. But this was just as bad, if not worse. There was something wrong, and he couldn't think what it was. Then it struck him: the thin lips held an old man's scowl, but the parchment skin was so thin, and stretched so tightly, that the skull showed plainly underneath, and the skull, like all skulls, was grinning. For the mouth was not collapsed and toothless as one might expect, but instead possessed every tooth, sharply defined. The effect was unpleasant and unsettling.

The girl asked him something, providing a welcome diversion. He answered, and then, feeling that he had waited long enough for the requirements of politeness to be met, asked a question of his own on a subject he had been thinking of before but hadn't wanted to broach at that time.

"Do you have any sisters or brothers? Or do you live alone here with..." He indicated the old man with a movement of his eyes.

"Oh yes," she answered eagerly. "I have a sister and two brothers. Elspeth is my big sister. She's five years older than me. I wish you could meet her. She's so nice!"

He pressed on, innocently. "Does she live here too, or did she move away?"

"Well..." she hesitated, as if unsure of how to proceed, then more confidently, "She loved the sound of the falls, you see. She used to sit for hours on the high ledge near the top, and just listen to the falls." Confidingly, "The falls talk, you know, but she understood it better than I did then. I guess I was too young. She said that a young man lived in the falls, and that he kept asking her to come and live with him. Sometimes she stayed there all day, talking to him. One time she didn't come home. Da found her in the morning, floating in the big whirlpool under the falls. She was lying face down in the water, going round and round, round and round..." Her voice was soft and dreamy, not at all sad. Then she brightened and said, "Of course that was only her body. You see she had gone to live with the young man in the falls. The very next night I could hear her voice, calling me to come and stay with them. But I couldn't you know. I had to take care of the others. They needed me." She sat quietly with her hands folded, lost in reverie.

Father sat there stunned. He had a particular aversion to people whose minds were in any way twisted. Not just eccentric—that, he rather enjoyed—but those who had lost contact with reality.

As he remarked to me, "Here was I, one moment talking to a sensible young woman in a perfectly normal way; the next, I was sitting there, miles from nowhere, between a living skeleton and a crazy woman!"

And the "living skeleton" chose that moment to croak, "That's right."

Shaken more than he cared to admit, he decided to ignore what he had just heard, and to bring the conversation back to safer ground. "What about your brothers? Do they live here with you?"

She came back abruptly from wherever her thoughts had taken her.

"Well," she said, her tone regretful. "My brother Timothy isn't like the rest of us. He doesn't like it here. But he has a boat and he comes with supplies once in a while. He never stays long, though." She brightened again. "Leopold though, my oldest brother Leo, he stayed. Leo was the painter in the family; the artist, I guess I should say. He was always drawing and painting pictures. Ma says that when Leo was only five years old, he could draw a face so that you could know who it was. His paintings of Da and Great-Gramma are so like them you'd think they were really there, looking out at you. He was a wonderful painter."

He noted the use of the word "was," when applied to Leo, and had a premonition that he wasn't going to like what he was going to hear.

She continued, eager to communicate. "One day Leo decided to climb to the top of the cliffs up behind here, to get a different view to paint. He took his things, and climbed up and up and up. He was very strong, almost as strong as Uncle or Da even." (Father thought of those sheer rock faces, and marvelled. He knew that he wouldn't have attempted them.) "But, he forgot to ask permission of Old Woman who lives in the mountain, and she pushed him off. That afternoon, Ma seemed to sense something. She and Leo were very close, and she knew. She told Uncle and Da to go and look for him. I was just young then, ten or eleven I think, but I wanted to go, and they let me. We found him up where the creek flows along below the cliffs, sitting in the water between two rocks. One of his arms was moving in the current, just as if he was drawing! He had the most odd little smile on his face."

For a moment she was silent, remembering. Then, "Most of his head was gone. We buried him up on the hill, where you could look out across the water. But of course, he was in the falls then, too. I heard him there that night, singing."

This story affected him strongly. Too strongly. There was a part of his mind that was an observer, cool, remote, who noticed his perceptions were altered. For one thing, there was a halo around the lamp that should not have been there, of a colour that he could never remember, if it was a colour. The air in the room seemed heavy, almost as if he was underwater. The rest of him wished he was back in his boat, heading away from there.

She was saying, "I was very angry with Old Woman for pushing him off. Great-Gramma explained to me how it was that Old Woman had to do it, but I was still angry for a long time. We were going to be married, you see, when I was a year older."

He thought he must have misunderstood something. "But I thought you said he was your brother?"

"Yes, that's right, my oldest brother, Leo."

He didn't know what to say. He was very confused. In that time and place, incest was a taboo so strict as to be never mentioned by civilized people. Yet she seemed so innocent... It was impossible to condemn her.

He had had enough. He began to assemble reasons as to why he must leave. It wasn't easy. She was so happy to have someone to talk with, and the night was still young.

There was movement over by the stove. Uncle croaked his "That's right," and began to get out of the big chair. Up, he rose, and up—and up—. The figure that Father had assumed was a wizened little old man was huge! Even shrunken with age as he must have been, he was at least six feet tall, with broad shoulders and massive chest that made his giant hands seem almost normal. Without looking around, he strode slowly and majestically across the room and through a door in the dividing wall, the hands held before him as if they were leading the way. The girl must have noticed from Father's expression that he was disturbed. She said hesitantly, "Uncle is alright. He's changed some in the last year or two, but you don't need to worry, he probably doesn't even know you're here. There is one thing. I don't even know if I should even mention it..." Then decisively, "I guess I should, though. If I was you, I wouldn't let him get behind me."

That was enough for him. He thought, "That's it. That's enough. I'm off!"

He began to make excuses, pleading tiredness, having to check the boat tie-ups, anything. But, as he had feared, it wasn't going to be easy. She was determined that he should stay.

"Oh," she insisted, "you must stay for supper. I've had no one to talk to for so long. Please stay!"

I am sure that he could not have resisted. Chivalry, sympathy, and just a touch of male vanity would have proved too strong. But it was not for him to decide. There came the sound of chain rattling, a thunderous "a-woof," and the sound of a heavy door closing. His hostess relaxed visibly, as if something had been decided.

"There," she said. "That's settled. You can't leave now. Thunder is out, and he won't let us lock him up until morning. I couldn't protect you out there in the nighttime, and Uncle, well, he just wouldn't care, that's all."

Father considered this. Normally, a vicious dog wouldn't deter him once he had decided on a course of action. When he put on his "command" voice and said, "Go on, get out of here!" they usually got. Those few that didn't, found that they faced a more vicious predator than themselves, one armed with a rock, a stick or a clutching pair of powerful hands. But that bark had come from no ordinary chest and throat; it was dark, and discretion might be good advice. He had been more than half decided to stay anyhow. It is evidence of his disorientation that there should have been any question as to what he should do. The prospect of a good meal and an evening of conversation with a beautiful young woman who listened attentively to his every word would normally have reconciled Father to far stranger surroundings than these. So now, however reluctant he may have been, it was not as bad as it might seem that he was forced by circumstances to do what he at least partially wanted to do anyway, so he accepted her invitation as graciously as if the choice had been entirely his own.

He settled himself, determined to relax and make the best of the evening. Tabitha was looking calmly at him from the woodbox whence she had returned when he rose to leave, and he felt a little ashamed of his apprehensions. But then Uncle came stalking back from wherever he had been, his face under the wisps of hair looking more skull-like than before. He lowered himself into his chair, joint by joint, and placed the huge spider-hands on his thighs where they clung once again in that disturbing semblance of sentient things. Then he turned his head and looked directly and malevolently at the young man across from him.

Just for a moment their eyes locked, then he turned again to his previous position and became utterly still.

No sign of breathing stirred his chest. Father was left in no doubt at all, Uncle knew there was a stranger in his house, and he was extending no welcome.

No, he certainly would not let Uncle get behind him. No warning had been needed.

The girl bustled about, stirring up the fire, setting the table; all the "homey" things that dispel bad thoughts and soothe ruffled nerves. He dragged his self-confidence back from wherever it had fled, and the cool voice in the back of his mind asked derisively what it had been afraid of. Some poor old man near his last days, fingers twisted with rheumatism? But the other presence refused to be convinced, and conjured up ancient superstitions, and ancestral fear of the dark. And as it looked nervously out of the corners of his eyes for nameless shadow-things, the cool, calm voice was silent. And soon, in accordance with the old saying that "If you look for trouble, you likely will find it," the view from the corner of his eyes revealed something very disturbing. When seen at the extreme reach of peripheral vision, Uncle's face and head appeared totally fleshless, nothing more than a naked grinning skull to which adhered a few tufts of lank grey hair! Startled, Father jerked his head around to look squarely at this apparition, but in full view it was once again only an old man that sat there, the flesh on his face thin and taut, but quite evident. The girl asked him some question and he turned to answer her, but he couldn't prevent his attention slipping back to the edge of vision. There once more, was the grisly skull with shadowed sockets and grinning lipless mouth!

Determined to reassert control, he shifted his chair so that the old man was near his centre of vision. It worked well enough, but the remembrance of what he thought he had seen had no good effect on his nerves.

In an effort to re-establish an atmosphere of normal conversation, he asked, "Have you lived here all your life? Haven't you ever gone out where there are people?"

"Oh no, never. This is good enough for me. I'd never leave here. Why, I couldn't bear to go where I couldn't hear the falls!"

Not wanting to hear any more about the falls, he went hastily on. "Am I really the only visitor you've ever had?"

She didn't answer for a moment. Then, "Well, there was one other. Though I don't really think I should call him a visitor. His boat was drifting along one day out on the water. I took the canoe and went out to see who it was, and what they were doing. He needed something for his engine, and he asked me if we might have it. I told him that if he could get to shore he could ask Da or Uncle. So he paddled his boat over and anchored it. He was lucky it was nice and calm that day. Da was in an awful temper about it. He said I shouldn't let strangers know about us. And Uncle wouldn't talk to him at all."

He waited for her to continue, but when she showed no sign of doing so, he asked, "What happened? How did he get away?"

She considered the question for quite a while, then, "I don't know. Perhaps he didn't. His boat is out there in the water by the mouth of the creek. I didn't like him. He was ugly. Not at all nice like you are."

The flattery, if it was that, was lost on Father. All that he could think of was that the only other visitor to this place had either left without his boat, or was still there. He remembered the seaweed on the sunken cabin. It had been there for a long time. Unbidden, the thought came: perhaps the stranger had let Uncle get behind him! He wished the thought had stayed unborn. He wondered how it could be that she wouldn't know. Was she lying?

For the last while, the room had been filled with the delicious aroma of frying ham, and now at last, dinner was ready. Ham, bread fried in the pan after the ham was cooked, biscuits with dripping for butter, and a dish of greens and some roots that he didn't recognize. And of course tea, which he refused as diplomatically as possible.

"Just water please, if you don't mind. Tea at supper-time upsets my stomach," he lied.

"Oh no, I don't think this tea will do that to you."

But he was adamant, so she brought him a glass of water.

As she was putting the food on the table, he asked, "What about the others?"

"Oh, they're all right. I fed them just before you came. They have an egg in a glass of goat's milk. Sometimes I put honey in for a treat. They'll have another at bedtime, or something else nourishing that they can drink."

Straight from the stories of his youth, but no more

welcome for that, came the thought, "Something warm perhaps, and red?"

This dredging up of bits from childhood horror stories was new to his experience. He thought that the tea must surely be to blame. Whatever the cause, this struggle between the rational part of him and the primitive, fuelled by the brooding, skeletal figure on one side and the familiar comfortable kitchen on the other was disturbingly unpleasant.

There were biscuits and honey, and wild berry preserves. Tabitha strolled over from her woodbox, begged prettily for the scraps, and her presence tipped the balance back almost to normal. He relaxed a little.

Then dinner was over, the dishes were cleared away and the time came for more serious conversation. After awhile, the girl started to talk of the falls, and how much it meant to her to have it for company.

"Would you like to listen to it? This would be a good time."

Before he could think of an excuse, she had picked up the lamp and started to cross the room, leaving him the choice of following her or remaining in the dark with Uncle. An easy decision!

She led him into the room behind the chimney. It was indeed a living room with fireplace. Solid-looking furniture was visible in the soft light of the lamp, and pictures in ornate gold frames hung on the walls. There were many curious objects on a low round table in the centre of the room and on the well-filled bookcases.

There was a window with closed curtains of some dark colour. He had not much time to examine details as she walked quickly across to a pair of large glass doors which she pushed open, and he followed her onto a wide veranda. He saw a white-painted railing on lathe-turned uprights, and beyond it only night and some dim sky. There were a few wooden chairs scattered about.

She turned down the lamp and placed it behind some bulky object near the wall, so they were in almost total darkness. He was immediately conscious that Uncle was somewhere in that darkness, and not necessarily in the chair where they had left him, but there was some light reflecting from the wall and his eyes soon adjusted enough that he thought he would be able to see anyone approaching.

"Listen," she whispered softly. "If you listen carefully and are lucky, they may talk to you."

They stood in silence for a while, and the falls did make sounds like voices calling; strange, eerie song-like sounds. They would have been hypnotic, he thought, had he been less concerned about what lurked in the dark silent rooms behind, below and above him.

At last she sighed, retrieved the lamp and turned up the wick. She didn't seem inclined to talk, and he remained silent. They went back into the big living room, and this time he noticed a piano against the wall by the fireplace. As a musician and music lover he exclaimed, "That's quite a piano. It must have been some job to get that up the trail!"

She shook her head. "Oh no, Da and Uncle carried it up by themselves. I don't think they had any trouble."

The instrument was a massive upright of some very dark wood, with heavy solid ends instead of legs, the whole deeply carved. He thought that the average man probably couldn't have lifted one end of it off the floor, and his respect for the strength once possessed by the old skeleton in the chair increased sharply.

He asked, "Do you play?"

"No, Da is the piano player in the family. He taught me to sing a bit. He likes to hear me sing when he plays. He told me that I could be a great singer if I left here and went across the sea. But I just don't want to."

There was an oval plate about two feet long mounted on its edge on top of the piano. It depicted, in the most incredible detail, a huge crab, claws raised in defiance. So striking was the design and colour that he immediately felt a great desire to own it. It was the only one of the strange objects in the room that he remembered clearly. She held the light up toward the fireplace so that it shone on a gold-framed portrait.

"This is one of Leo's paintings of Great-Gramma when she was young."

The painting was one of those that catch and hold the eye. It was of a very old woman, hands and face wrinkled and creased. She was mostly in shadow, but what could be seen seemed to suggest more than a portrait in good light would have revealed. She was smiling, but it was not a friendly smile. Her eyes were deeply shadowed, except for two tiny blood-red flecks where the pupils should have been. The effect was powerful and quite disturbing.

She moved on, held up the lamp again. She said,

"This is Da."

He forgot Great-Gramma, even his sense of where he was, so great was the impact of what he saw.

Over a strong jaw, clean-shaven, the man's mouth stretched wide and thin-lipped; grim, uncompromising, unforgiving. High cheekbones and a broad, high brow, a swept back mane of pure white hair, and the eyes, the glowing yellow eyes, blazing down on him like fire! Here was a man who might have started a religion, or a war, founded an empire, or destroyed one. The mind behind that face must have been one of extraordinary power. There was that focus, that intentness, which only great strength can command.

Now he understood why the house was built as it was. This man had willed it so, and difficulty had no meaning. But why would such a man be hiding here, on this remote shore, fearing or loathing strangers?

Such was the impression that face made on him, that try as he would, he could recall nothing else of what the room contained. Once pinned by those terrible eyes, nothing else mattered!

(Leo must have been an artist of exceptional genius. Father was not one to be easily awed or impressed by a portrait.)

She lowered the lamp, turning as she did so, but two glints of yellow seemed to still glow on the wall behind her. Shaken more than he cared to admit by a mere picture, he asked, "Where is your father? I'd like to meet him. Perhaps he'd play for me."

This was not true. He most decidedly did not want to meet the man whose image looked out of that picture, and the notion of him sitting down to the piano to play a few songs was too ridiculous to contemplate. What he wanted, and expected—for the man in that picture was surely not one who would hide from an intruder— was for her to tell him that her father was away on a trip somewhere. He was not at all prepared for what she did say.

"Oh no," she exclaimed, obviously flustered "You couldn't, I mean, it isn't possible..." she paused, "you see Da has been dead now for nearly two years."

The room seemed to whirl a bit, and he thought, unsteadily, hadn't she said "plays," and "likes" and so on? He wanted to ask, but felt she wouldn't answer, and he didn't want that to happen, though he didn't know why.

As they returned to the kitchen, he sneaked a sly glance at Uncle's face. Two slivers of glacial blue glared balefully back at him. That came as a relief. He feared they would be yellow, although what difference that would have made, he couldn't say.

Once again seated at the table, talk seemed to lag a bit. His companion seemed pensive, and he wondered what the voices had said to her. After a bit, he asked— greatly daring, for he feared the answer might once again be not to his liking—"You mention others. Who else lives here with you?"

"Well, of course there's Ma. She's a bit strange, I sup- pose. She never leaves her room. She's fun to talk to though, she thinks she's a girl again. She thinks that she's younger than me, but of course she knows so much more. There's no use you trying to talk with her.

You don't fit into her memory, and she wouldn't know you were there. At least, I think it works like that. It's how Great-Gramma explained it to me. And then there's Great-Gramma herself. She's very strange. I don't quite know how to tell you. She hates the light now, and she only leaves her room when the house is dark. I haven't actually seen her for a long time."

She was thoughtful for a while, then suddenly, "I don't really think I would like to see Great-Gramma in the light now, though I'm not sure why. Of course, you mustn't—I mean, there's no light, so..." She stammered to a stop. "And that's all, I guess."

He wondered, "I guess? Surely she must know. What in the world is going on here?"

She rose and went over to the sink, and taking a large pitcher from an outside cooler, poured some of its contents into a mug, which she set on the arm of Uncle's chair by his knee. Then she put the pitcher and some glasses into a basket, lit another lamp and said, "It's time for their bedtime drink. You'll be all right here. I won't be long."

Upon which, taking lamp and basket, she disappeared through the other door, leaving him alone with Uncle. As she went, he noticed that there were three glasses. She had not told him the truth. With uncanny timing came the croak, "That's right!" It seemed almost as if the old man could read his thoughts. The dour face looked amused; behind it the skull grinned maniacally.

Turning his chair toward the stove, Father planted his feet firmly, stared intently at Uncle, and silently dared him to turn into a skeleton.

The old house creaked. The clock ticked. A log in the stove collapsed, causing him to jump, and he realized that his nerves were in very bad shape. The lamp flame flickered wildly for no apparent reason, as lamps do. He willed it to stay lit. The wick needed trimming but he dared not touch it. What if it went out? He made sure of the match box in his pocket, considered, then took out a match and placed it on the table, feeling a bit sheepish as he did so. Tabitha jumped from the woodbox, and walking daintily over to him, rubbed her cheek against his knee and purred. Illogically, this made him feel better.

At last the girl came back. As she passed Uncle's chair, she picked up his mug and took it to the sink. It was empty!

He told me, "Now that was, in a way, the worst thing that had happened to me in that house. It just wasn't possible. I was watching that old man every moment of the time. He simply couldn't have emptied that mug without me seeing him do it. Yet, I saw her fill it. I still can't figure it out. Something wasn't right there, and old skull-face was part of it."

She put the pitcher back in the cooler and washed the mug. The glasses had been left where they had been taken. She went to the stove and fed it a log, then, after blowing out the other lamp, came and sat in the chair facing him. Tabitha jumped up and settled comfortably in her lap.

"Now we can talk. What shall we talk about?"

"Tell me about yourself. How it was to grow up here.

What you thought about, and what you did."

She smiled happily, and he realized that never before in her life had anyone been interested in what she thought. Not in this family, with the possible exception of her sister, and perhaps—because of the age difference—not even her.

She began slowly, hesitantly, but soon gaining confidence, became eager, even fluent, though occasionally using words with which he was not familiar. It was one of the strangest accounts he had ever heard—perhaps the most strange of all. For what she told him was a mixture of legend and reality that was like some fantastic dream. Her world from as far back as she could remember, was peopled by spirits, by talking animals and birds, by Powers and Forces, good and evil, and sometimes not either. And what was perhaps most surprising to him was that here, for the only other time in his life, he heard names from the mythos of Charlie, "The Old Indian," whose mountain tribe had died off many years ago, and whose legends—as far as he knew—were not shared with any other people. Here once more were Spotted Woman, White Bear, who became the moon, and Man-Who-Could-Not-Die.

They all lived for this wild girl, for whom life and imagination were inextricably mingled. Where could she have heard of them? He suddenly remembered the picture of the old woman with the red-flecked eyes. She must have been—must be—of Charlie's tribe, older even than he was. She could have left before the epidemic that destroyed them. It explained the exotic beauty of the girl, one of those fortuitous combinations of races. It explained the familiarity with herbs and roots unknown to Europeans. Great-Gramma had recounted the legends, used them to explain thunder and lightning, the wind and the rainbow, and why animals behaved as they did.

The girl, infinitely receptive, had accepted this version of reality: why should she not? On its own terms it made sense, and in her mind it had no competition whatsoever. For her, the world he knew was the legend. What could be more obviously mythical than that world as pictured in the little pile of *Ladies Home Journals* he had seen on the corner table near the door? He thought it probable that none of the members of her family would have had time or inclination to educate a small girl. To be fair, they may have thought that living here, it could only confuse her, and that she would never need it.

So he listened entranced, as she took him back to a world as it may have been before the Europeans had intruded, to a mythos now lost, and never to be regained. One more complex, more attuned to nature, more satisfying than that which had displaced it. He realized now that the girl was not only not insane, but quite possibly more sane and more in tune with her surroundings than he was himself.

It was with a real sense of loss that he heard her pause, then exclaim, "My, look how late it is. I've never talked so much in my whole life! I'd better show you to your room."

For he knew that he would never enter that world again, and—so unfamiliar was it to his reality—that even the memory would grow dim. This world into which he had peered so briefly had stirred something deep within him. He felt akin to it, and wished that he had listened more closely to the stories old Charlie had told so long ago. And the gaunt presence across the room chose just this moment to croak once again his "That's right." Could he hear thoughts?

Taking up the lamp, she led him across the room into a hallway, then upstairs into another hall. She pointed to her left. "There's a bathroom just over there."

The room into which she led him was a corner one, with a window on each outer wall. Lighting a lamp that was on a little table near the bed, she looked around thoughtfully, remarking with less conviction than he would have liked, "I guess you'll be all right here. Good night!" With that she turned and left him, closing the door behind her. He listened to the sound of receding footsteps, then re-opened the door and padded cat-silent to the bathroom, with the thought that it might be better to visit there before his presence was noticed.

Back in the bedroom, he closed the door firmly. It was solid and strong, but there was no lock or latch. Much to his relief, he found a sturdy chair that fitted under the door handle, the famous "traveller's lock." He noticed that the room smelled musty, faintly unpleasant. Both windows were warped, but he succeeded in forcing the one that faced the ravine. This let in the sound of the falls, which he hadn't previously noticed. It seemed a bit more friendly than before—less alien. He inspected the room more closely. Not that there was much to see: a heavy bed, a few chairs, a closet, which he opened cautiously, lamp in hand. There were a few items of clothing draped on hangers and a pair of men's boots, worn and white with mould. He checked the walls—they were sound—and closed the door. Going back to the bed he put the lamp on the table and turned down the bed-cover.

The unpleasant odour grew stronger. Lifting the sheet to his face, he breathed deeply, then wished he hadn't. There was a bad component to the smell; something unhealthy. The notion came to him that someone had died here in this bed, and he instantly resolved that there was no chance of him even sitting on it, much less sleeping there. He replaced the covers, tucking them in firmly to keep the odour from escaping and went to the window to breathe some fresh air. From far below, the creek made that pleasant, familiar sound he knew so well, a pleasure somewhat marred by the realization of how far down it was to the source, and the memory of those frail-looking pilings that held the weight of the house.

He listened for a time to the falls, but it spoke in no language he knew, and his thoughts dwelt more inside the house than out. Turning from the window, he placed the most comfortable-looking chair in the centre of the room facing the door, and settled into it. It would be a long night, for he was determined that he would not sleep. Even so, he may have dozed off a bit, sitting there. He couldn't be certain, but he knew that something heard but not remembered had brought him back to full alertness. The house was tomb-quiet, but all his senses were on edge, and he was sure the cause was not his imagination.

He was looking straight at the door as the handle began to turn almost noiselessly, only the faintest rasp of metal on wood betraying the motion. The small, cool observer in his mind protested, "Oh no, this is too much. It's straight out of one of our ghost story books, the door handle always turns noiselessly!" Just then, there was a slight squeak of metal on dry wood, and a quiet click from the handle mechanism. It served to thoroughly dispel the feeling of unreality that had kept him from reacting. There was someone out there in the hallway behind that door, trying to get into the room without alerting him, and he doubted their purpose was to pay him a friendly visit.

Rising quietly, he took two steps and seized the most solid chair in the room. Its heavy legs started square at the seat and tapered to round. One of them would make a fine club. He raised it high overhead, ready to smash it on the floor if the door gave way and he didn't like what came through it. The door handle had turned as far as it would go. There was a pause, then the door moved inward slightly as if from a push, but the chair held firmly. The handle began to rotate back again, just as slowly and smoothly, making the same click, the same dry squeak. The door-knobs were small, and the chair back exerted considerable pressure on the shaft. It was no frail hand that tried that door! Once more the chair moved as pressure was applied, and again it held. He stood there tense and ready, but the minutes passed uneventfully, and he decided that the caller had departed. He put the chair quietly back on the floor, and discovered that his shirt was clammy with sweat.

He told me, "It's one thing to read that sort of story in a book, but it's an entirely different matter to stand there in the middle of the night trapped in a house that might have any sort of crazy person roaming around in it. It has a wonderful way of concentrating your mind." (I don't know if he'd ever read Samuel Johnson's comments on hanging.)

The house was silent again. From the open window came soothing noises from the creek and falls, and the sense of menace faded. He settled into his chair, still facing the door, and this time felt in no danger of dozing off. Relaxing a bit, but still alert, he thought, "Now, if this was in one of the books we used to read, the piano would be sure to start playing." But the only sounds were those of an old house in the night. Perhaps a few more than usual because of its size and the way it was built. The sound of the falls grew louder, perhaps carried to him by a stray drift of wind, and again he felt he could almost hear voices in it. Not words, but that eerie wordless singing he had heard before, and in spite of his resolve, he might have been lulled once more into the world it sang of, if he had not been brought back instantly to attention by the sound of the piano!

Someone was playing the old song "Home Sweet Home," but however familiar it may have been, heard there in the night in that room where the lamp flame made the shadows move, the effect on him was profound.

"I felt the hair rise up on the back of my neck," he said. "I guess that piano hadn't been tuned since it had been brought there, and it sounded like something from another world. I suppose if I'd heard it anywhere else, I'd have thought it sounded terrible, but it seemed to fit right in, hearing it there."

After the refrain, the pianist played the tune once again, but this time embellished with ornamental figures; cascades of rippling runs, trills and chords such as he had never heard or imagined, and all the while the simple tune played on undisturbed. At last it stopped and the house was still. Without warning, a crashing discord shattered his mood and the pianist began to play something so strange and compelling that he could never forget it, but so complex that he could never describe it. The music sang and stormed, and grieved, and held him spellbound. He couldn't believe that human hands and fingers could be capable of such things as he was hearing. (He had never heard a concert pianist.) He felt a great desire to sneak down the stairs to snatch a glimpse of the person who could accomplish such a marvel, but he thought he knew who it must be, and the chance that he might meet those blazing eyes face to face put an end to that notion. The music ended with a savage crescendo of octaves down the entire length of the keyboard, which resolved into thunderous chords that seemed to shake the very walls. In the silence that followed, he realized that he had heard something very odd. Somehow, the pianist—who he was certain was also the composer—had contrived to fit his music to the state of the instrument, so that being out of tune enhanced the effect instead of damaging it. (I am not at all sure how this might be done, or if it is indeed possible, but Father had an excellent ear and played several instruments, so I am inclined to accept his word on it.)

There was another silence, lasting perhaps for as much as five minutes or so. Then came another tune that Father knew well, having played it many times himself. It was "The Last Waltz," that sad little song that used to be played at the end of every night of dancing. It was played unembellished; simply, affectingly. It ended, and this time the silence remained unbroken.

He sat there, thinking deeply, more affected than he would have thought possible. Was there a message, perhaps a warning, in the choice of songs? It was not a comforting thought, and he tried not to dwell on it. He believed he knew now why the girl had spoken as she did about her "Da," and who the extra glass was for. Just under two years ago that too-intense mind had finally burned itself out. Sanity fled, never to return. To the girl's mind, the "Da" she knew, had died, yet still lived on. Thus the confusion of tenses. He walked the house at night, like Great-Gramma. Father wondered, had it been his hand that tried the door? He shuddered, but reconsidering, thought that it was not. That one would not be stopped by a mere locked door. It was probable that he often played the piano in the night, and thus, it was quite natural that it should happen this night. Did he sit by day at the window under the peaked roof, watching over the water for someone, something, that he feared? Whatever it was, if that man and his savage brother feared it, Father knew that he would not care to meet it.

Satisfied with his speculations, he settled in to await the morning. It was now two o'clock and there would be about four hours more until daylight. He felt that they would be uneventful, but that didn't stop him from putting the heavy chair where he could quickly reach it.

There was to be yet one more event that night, a small thing, but it upset him greatly, and the memory of it would haunt him at odd moments for the rest of his days. About three o'clock, that hour of the early morning in which people are at their most vulnerable, he rose, stretched, and then went to the window to listen once more to the falls.

As he neared the opening, he heard a strange sound, so faint that it could have been going on for some time covered by the sound of the running water. He leaned out, listening. He could hear it clearly now. It was someone crying. Desolate, infinitely mournful, the sound of one for whom hope was withered, forever gone; of blighted dreams, immeasurable sadness. It kept on and on, sometimes almost inaudible, never loud. Faint as it was, it was more than he could bear to listen to and he went back into the room until he could hear it no more. He felt a strong impulse to seek out whoever it was and console them, for he had a very tender heart for suffering. But thinking of what he had heard, he knew that whoever it was was beyond comforting, beyond any consolation he could offer. After a bit, he went back to the window, for it was somehow worse to think it was going on unheard than for him to actually hear it. But it had stopped, and though he stayed there for some time, it did not start again. He wondered if it was the woman that Melody had called "Ma," who had awakened to find that she was not a young girl, but withered, old and alone; her sons gone and her man insane. Or (for the voice had been sexless and could have been either woman or man), might it have been the last visitor? Trapped, held there for years, for purposes it might be well not to know about. After all, Great-Gramma had surely outlived her normal span of years, by any normal measure. He pushed the morbid thoughts from him with revulsion. He would not think that the beautiful young woman whose company he had so enjoyed could be party to any such plot. Going back at last to his chair, he settled in to wait for morning.

Before long, the signs he knew so well heralded its approach. The birds, the lightening of the sky, and then the welcome sight of sunlight on the distant mountain tops. He felt secure then, and dozed there, upright in the chair. A thunderous "A-woof" and the sound of a door shutting woke him. He rose, stretched, removed the chair from under the door-knob and went down the hall.

Back in his room, he hadn't waited long before there came a knock on the door and the girl's cheery voice called, "Oh Mr. Hammond, are you awake?" He followed her down the stairs and into the kitchen, noting with relief that Uncle was absent. There was a breakfast of hotcakes and syrup waiting for him, and when he sat, Tabitha greeted him like an old friend, jumped onto his lap and purred.

Melody had more questions to put to him about "the outside." He answered as well as he could, if not always to her satisfaction. For instance, she wanted to know how big a "city" was, how many people usually lived in one. "A hundred? Five hundred?" Then greatly daring, "A thousand? Surely not that many!" Guessing wildly, he told her that the nearest city to them—Vancouver—had nearly fifty thousand people living there. She was shocked at first, but then relaxed and said, laughing merrily, "You are a mischief. For a moment there I almost took you seriously!"

At last came the time when he said he must be on his way, and this time he remained firm in spite of her entreaties. She gave in graciously, and walked with him down the trail. Untying the skiff, he asked if she needed anything that he might be able to supply.

"No-o-o," she answered thoughtfully, "Timmy will be by one of these days." Then, "Oh, but there is one thing. If you had any raisins—we're out of raisins."

Now, raisins were something that Father always had in good supply for the rice puddings which were one of his favourite dishes. He jumped into the skiff and in moments was back with an unopened box of raisins. She was so delighted that he wished he had brought two boxes, until she said, "I'm so glad you had some. Uncle likes raisins so much, and we were right out of them."

He pictured those skeleton teeth grinding on his raisins, and drew no pleasure from the spectacle. But he consoled himself with the knowledge that he had made Melody happy.

She untied the shore line and threw the end to him. They said good-bye; she told him to stop again if he was ever near, that he would always be welcome. Back on the boat, he coiled the shoreline, pulled the skiff onto the stern, hauled up the anchor. The engine started on the first turn. He eased the clutch lever forward and swung the wheel until the bow pointed to the far shore. He turned and waved to Melody, and she waved back vigorously. When he had gone half a mile or so, he looked back for one last time. She was still standing there, just visible against the rocks.

"I felt a bit sad," he said. "I don't know why. She seemed happy enough to be where she was. But I thought that it wasn't right somehow, her there all alone with those old people, all of them at least half-crazy one way or another. She should have had someone young for company. I hoped that her brother might bring a young man for a visit, perhaps to live there when the old ones died. No one who saw that girl would ever want to leave her. Of course," he added hastily "I was already spoken for!"

As the boat glided smoothly through the still water, he thought about what he had experienced. There were still things that troubled him. If her father and uncle were so secretive, why hadn't they pushed the sunken boat out into deep water rather than leave it there to draw attention? Why was Melody so unfamiliar with the world outside? Surely her brother Timothy could have answered her questions. As he mused on these and other things, time passed quickly.

About twenty miles along his way, he rounded a

point of land which sheltered a float with a boat tied to it, and a smallish house on the shore behind. At the sound of his engine, three people ran out of the house and stood waving at him to stop. There was an older man, the usual worn-looking woman, and a young man who appeared to be their son.

As he pulled in to the float, they were there to greet him, the older two both speaking at once with fairly heavy Swedish accents. He eventually understood that their boat engine had broken down. They had to replace a part, and was he by any chance going as far as Lund, where they might get a new one, or have one made? He was, and after a bit of discussion among the trio, and leave-taking, the older man came onto the boat carrying the broken part. After a few hours of travel, as conversation began to lag, Father asked the man, "Have you lived long in this part of the country?"

"Well, let's see now, we moved up here just before the war, in nineteen-twelve, or was it eleven? Something like that."

"So I guess you would know just about every one who lives around here?"

The other affirmed that he not only knew everyone who lived within thirty miles of there that had a house, but that he knew the name of their boat, dog, cat or horse, if they had any!

"So who is the family that lives...?" and he described roughly where he had landed. The man shook his head in negation.

"Who told you anyone lived on that shore? Never was anyone there. Probably never will be. Nothing there but rock and salal brush."

It was the answer that he expected. He changed the subject without answering the question.

Time passed. Father's work kept him in the area bounded roughly by Jervis Inlet, Pender Harbour and Campbell River. He made no more trips north, until one day a friend wanted desperately to go to Church House and no one would take him there on such short notice. He came to Father, who consented without too much urging.

It was summer, the weather was fine, and he had nothing to do that couldn't be put off. The trip was uneventful, but once he was back there among the islands and inlets, he thought again of the girl with the golden eyes and her strange family. Without hesitating, he swung the wheel as if he had planned it that way and headed back toward that bleak shore and the house he remembered so well. Gradually traffic on the water thinned, until at last there was no sign of human activity at all. The sun was near the mountain tops as he neared the cove where he had picked up the man whose engine had broken. He decided to spend the night there, not wishing to reach his destination in the dark. As he pulled into the cove, he saw the place was deserted. There was no boat. The float was more than half sunken, and a tree branch hung out of the window of the house. He tied up to the float. The light was fading rapidly, and he decided not to go ashore. It would be a gloomy place in the dusk. It would speak to him of lost hopes, despair and hard work with small reward.

He made supper, and went to sleep quickly. Waking up at daybreak—as he always did—he breakfasted and cast off. By mid-morning he was at the shore where the house was concealed. The roof peak was not visible, but there was a bit of mist drifting above the shore and among the treetops, which he thought would probably hide it. As he drifted to a stop, he noticed that the sunken boat was gone, probably washed into deep water by a storm. Feeling an oppressive sense of foreboding, he dropped anchor and took a line ashore as before. The canoe was there, but held no water. Contact with the damp ground had rotted the thin hull; it would not float again. He ran lightly up the steep trail, now grass-covered, and almost invisible. Knowing what he would find, he broke through the fringe of bushes that almost blocked the way, and looked across the clearing. There was no sound, no sign of life. The house was gone. He went to the edge where it had been. There it was, or what was left of it, in the bottom of the ravine, an untidy heap of broken and charred boards and timbers, almost unrecognizable as having once been a house. A heap of something that may have been a piano lay on the rocks by the creek bed. There was nothing at all in the place where the house had once stood, just bare rock streaked with clay. The pilings had not been cemented, but placed in indentations in the rock. When they went they left no traces. He stood there on the bank edge, reconstructing in his mind what had happened.

From the seedlings already growing along the edge, he knew that at least a year, probably a year and a half, had gone by since the house had stood there. It had likely been winter: a heavy snowfall may have added tons of weight to the house. One of the pilings—partly rotted—had given way, leaving others to take the pressure; they had collapsed explosively. As the front of the house dropped, the piano would have slid across the floor and through the doors. The house somersaulting after it, driven by the weight of the snow, to smash upside down onto the creek-bottom a hundred feet below. The stone chimney and fireplace would have crashed through the floors, and the massive stove, kept hot because of the cold weather, would have exploded when it hit, causing the fire. That most of the dry old wood remained, indicated either heavy rain or snow at the time.

He thought of Melody, pinned perhaps in the burning house, and grimaced painfully, but then realized that no one would be likely to survive the destruction. He remembered how she had looked, and the music of her voice, and as he did, he became conscious of the sound of the falls.

He said, "The human mind is a very strange thing. As I stood there listening, there seemed to be a difference in the sound of the falls. The more I listened, the more I thought that I could hear her voice, singing out over all the rest. Of course, I knew all along, that it being midsummer, there was less water going over the falls, so the 'talking' wasn't drowned out by the roar. But sometimes the mind pays no attention to common sense."

For a long time he stood there, listening, remembering, but at last a slight noise from the fringe of bush beyond the clearing brought him back to attention. He felt that he was being watched. He knew that this is a common feeling under such circumstances, then remembered the monster-dog Thunder, and looked for a rock that would fit comfortably in his hand. This was his favourite close-range weapon. With it he had once killed with a single blow a dog that had gone insane on seeing its master buried

The noise did not recur. It could have been the goats. They would likely survive on their own for quite a while. He looked around carefully. There were no tracks on the ground. The chicken house had collapsed and there were no signs of its occupants, but the other shed was still upright. He walked over to it and pulled the door open. It was—as he had supposed—a tool house. There were saws, axes, hammers, various other tools, neatly hanging or leaning against the walls. They had seen a lot of use, but had been well-kept. He hated to see tools left to go to waste and considered a heavy hammer and a particularly well-balanced axe, but in the end, he left them and closed the door.

"You know that I am not a superstitious man," he told me, "but a man knows, if he knows anything, that there are lucky tools, and there are unlucky ones, and these didn't feel lucky to me," adding hastily, "It's all in the mind, you understand, but it's not any the less real for that."

He walked over to the edge and looked for a last time at the wreckage, and thought for a brief moment that he might climb down to seek a souvenir. One of the carvings perhaps, or even the plate with the crab on it he had so much admired. He rejected the idea almost before it was formed, afraid of what else he might find, and not ashamed to admit it. Turning away, he walked quickly back toward where the trail began.

Just as he was about to push into the screen of bushes, a squeaky sort of "mew-w-w" sounded from off to his right. It was Tabitha, crouched and ready to flee, eyeing him warily. She was obviously not a great huntress, for her hips and backbone jutted sharply under matted fur, but she had survived. He hunched down, making soothing noises and calling her name. Before long, she was in his arms, purring loudly enough for a cat twice her size.

Gone now were any hopes that Melody might have moved away, or otherwise have survived the destruction of her house. She would never have left Tabitha behind. Without a backward glance at the clearing in the trees, he pushed through the bushes and trotted quickly down the overgrown trail, carrying the little tabby cat—still purring—in his arms.

Those steep mountain valleys are swept periodically by freshets from the spring melt and frequent torrential rains. The wreckage would long since have been washed into the sea. Some shards of glass and fragments of pottery, perhaps a few piano keys under the moss, will be all that marks the place where a house once stood by the talking falls.